THE DEADLY PAST

Don't miss any of the chilling adventures!

SPOOKSVILLE

THE DEADLY PAST

Christopher Pike

Aladdin

NEW YORK   LONDON   TORONTO   SYDNEY   NEW DELHI

ALADDIN

An imprint of Simon & Schuster Children's Publishing Division
1230 Avenue of the Americas, New York, NY 10020
This Aladdin hardcover edition April 2016
Text copyright © 1996 by Christopher Pike
Jacket illustration copyright © 2016 by Vivienne To
Also available in an Aladdin paperback edition.

For information about special discounts for bulk purchases,
please contact Simon & Schuster Special Sales at 1-866-506-1949
or business@simonandschuster.com.
Jacket designed by Jessica Handelman
Interior designed by Mike Rosamilia
The text of this book was set in Weiss Std.
Manufactured in the United States of America 0316 FFG
2 4 6 8 10 9 7 5 3 1
Library of Congress Control Number 2014946982
ISBN 978-1-4814-1091-5 (hc)
ISBN 978-1-4814-1089-2 (pbk)
ISBN 978-1-4814-1092-2 (eBook)

1

THE HORROR STARTED WITHOUT WARNING.

Adam Freeman and his friends were not far from home when they were attacked, just a half mile north of Spooksville, in an area where they seldom went. The woods they had hiked through to get there were not nearly so thick as the others around Spooksville. Resting on top of a hill, they saw nothing but rocks, desolate valleys, and a few bushes. Sally Wilcox, who had led them to the spot, said it looked like the far side of the moon.

"I bet they used to do nuclear testing here," she said as they continued climbing to the top of a rocky bluff that gave them a view of the ocean and Spooksville itself. "That's why not much grows here."

"That's ridiculous," Cindy Makey replied, brushing her long blond hair back from her cute face. "The government only performs nuclear tests in Nevada."

Sally stared hard at her with brown eyes that matched her brown hair. "I wasn't talking about the U.S. government," she said. "Remember Spooksville used to be part of ancient Lemuria, which went under the Pacific Ocean more than twenty thousand years ago. New Agers believe the Lemurian culture was peaceful, but I know for a fact that they built just as many bombs as we have today."

"Like you would know," Cindy snapped.

"Bum does say that Lemuria really existed," Watch said tactfully. Watch was known for always wearing four watches and having no last name.

"I hate to disagree with Bum," Adam Freeman said, catching his breath and wiping the sweat from his face. Adam was the shortest one in the group, and very conscious of the fact. Yet he was also the group's leader. "But how come there isn't more evidence of Lemuria and Atlantis still lying around?"

"You heard what Bum said," Watch replied. "When the two lands warred, they completely wiped each other out. But Bum says that Lemuria and Atlantis were descendants of even more ancient cultures. I believe him. I think our history books are very limited in their scope."

"But do you really think this place used to be radio-active?" Cindy asked, uneasily glancing around. "If that's true, we shouldn't be here."

"Why?" Sally asked with a snigger. "Are you afraid you might mutate into a plain-looking girl?"

"It looks like that happened to you already," Cindy replied.

Watch raised his hand before the two girls could get going. "If there was radiation here," he said, "there would be no plant life at all. I don't think we have to worry about it."

Adam cocked his head to one side. "What's that funny sound?"

"I don't hear anything," Sally said before pausing to listen closely. Then a puzzled expression crossed her face. "It sounds like wind blowing through a nar-row valley."

Watch shook his head, as he also listened. "It sounds like a distant heartbeat to me." He scanned the area with his thick glasses. "But I don't see anything that could be making the sound. Do you guys?"

Cindy pointed. "What about that bird way over there?"

The brown bird to which Cindy was pointing

seemed to be flying over a mountain range far beyond Spooksville. This puzzled Adam who didn't understand how they could even see something as small as a bird at such a distance. The sharp peaks over which the bird swept were at least three miles away. Also, it was kind of a funny-looking bird, with a long pointed head and an especially wide wingspan. He shook his head as he stared at the creature.

"That can't be a bird," he said.

"Of course it's a bird," Sally said impatiently. "What else could it be? A plane?"

Watch—who didn't see very well even wearing his glasses—stared at the strange creature. "I think Adam is right," he said after a long pause. "That's much too big to be a bird."

Sally shielded her eyes from the glare of the sun. "How can you tell how big it is?" she asked. "It's so far away."

"That's our point," Adam said. "We shouldn't be able to see it from here."

The brown bird appeared to see them.

It turned in their direction. The peculiar sound grew louder.

"Whatever it is, it's definitely making the sound," Watch said. "And look how fast it's coming. Now it's twice as big as it was a minute ago."

Sally was getting worried. "No bird can fly that fast."

"So it can't be a bird," Cindy insisted.

Adam began to back up. "Let's argue about what it is later. Right now it's coming our way at high speed and it's big. I think we should take cover."

Sally slowly nodded. "It might be hungry."

Cindy giggled uneasily. "We're going to feel stupid running from a bird."

Watch had also begun to back up. "I would rather feel stupid than dead." He paused and squinted. The bird—or whatever it was—let out a screeching cry. It pulled in its wings and seemed to go into free fall, plunging toward them like a missile. Even Watch, who seldom showed any sign of fear, stammered as he spoke next. "That looks like a pterodactyl."

"What's that?" Cindy asked.

Sally gasped. "A dinosaur!"

Watch shook his head. "It's not technically a dinosaur. But it lived at the time of dinosaurs, and was just as deadly."

"But that's impossible!" Cindy cried.

"Nothing is impossible in this town!" Adam yelled. He grabbed Cindy by the arm and began to pull her backward. "Let's get out of here. Now!"

They half-ran and half-slid down the bluff into a

narrow valley. But then they became terribly confused. They each began to run in a separate direction, having no idea where to go. Adam stopped them.

"We have to find a cave!" he yelled.

"We passed one a few minutes ago," Sally cried, stopping, pointing. "It was back that way!"

Watch pointed in the opposite direction. "I thought it was that way. But we'll never make it that far. We have to find something closer."

They searched the area anxiously.

The pterodactyl screeched again. Now its leathery wings were clearly visible, as well as its huge mouth. The monster seemed to be coming at them at a hundred miles an hour. It would be on them in seconds. Already the creature was flexing its sharp claws. Adam knew they had to get out of the open.

"If we can find a rock overhang," Adam said, "it could stop the pterodactyl from swooping in and snatching one of us."

"No!" Sally protested. "We need a cave to be safe!"

Watch grabbed her arm this time. "Adam is right! We'll never make it back to that cave! There's an over-hang! Let's go to it!"

They took off for the far end of the narrow valley, which dead-ended at a wall with a sharp overhang that jutted twenty feet out from it. Unfortunately, the over-hang would be at least twenty feet over their heads. So it afforded little protection. As a group they pressed themselves against the limestone wall.

"I wish I had a hand laser," Watch said, staring up at the approaching monster.

"A strong stick might help," Adam said, spying one halfway up the side of the stone wall. He pointed. "I'll try for it."

The pterodactyl screeched a third time.

It was maybe five seconds away.

Sally grabbed Adam's arm and pulled him back against the wall. "Stay here, you nut!" she cried. "It'll kill you!"

Adam shook her off. "It will kill us all if we don't frighten it away." Glancing up at the pterodactyl once, he braced himself and then leapt toward the stick. The monster bird had incredible control of its seemingly wild plunge. It immediately veered toward Adam, who was just putting his hand on the stick. Suddenly the pterodactyl extended its massive wingspan, which was at least twenty feet across, to slow itself enough to grab Adam. Even so it was still traveling at high speed, and that may have been what saved Adam.

The creature tried to grab him but missed.

Sort of. The claw scraped Adam's right shoulder.

Adam felt a wave of searing pain.

Blood stained his shirt.

"Adam!" the others screamed.

The pterodactyl was making another pass at him. This time Adam could smell it—like a cloud of rotting vegetation—blowing over him. The creature was not coming so fast this time, but rather, seemed to be plotting its moves. Adam could see the hungry intelligence in its huge black and red eyes. Red saliva dripped from its mouth, and Adam wondered what it had eaten last, if it had been human.

"Get back here!" Watch yelled.

Yet even though Adam was in pain and bleeding, he still wanted the stick. He understood that they needed it in order to beat back the pterodactyl to reach real shelter. The overhang would not discourage the creature for long. It could always land, and peck at them with its long beak.

"Coming!" Adam shouted as he grabbed the stick. His wound was serious. Blood dripped on the ground in front of him as he bent over. But with the long hard stick in his hand he felt a wave of confidence. The pterodactyl wasn't going to scratch him again!

Too bad the monster didn't share his conviction.

The pterodactyl swept in again, its wide wings stirring up eye-stinging dust. In spite of its great size, the creature was remarkably agile. It must have been smart as well, because seeing Adam's stick, it went for that first. With one swipe of the monster's claws, Adam almost had his hard-won weapon ripped from his hand. Quickly Adam adjusted his strategy. He started swinging the stick frantically, rather than hoping to land one solid blow.

"Take that, you overgrown chicken!" he shouted as he struck at the pterodactyl. By chance, one blow caught the flying reptile on the top of the head and the thing let out a bloodcurdling scream.

"Kill it!" Cindy yelled from beneath the overhang.

"The pterodactyl probably thinks you're talking to him!" Sally shouted at him. "Get over here, Adam! Quit being such a hero!"

"You guys get to the cave!" he shouted back. "I'll keep it busy!"

"We're not leaving you!" Sally hollered. She turned to Watch and asked, "Should we leave him?"

Watch hesitated. "I hate to, but maybe we should. It could come after us any second, and we have only one stick."

"I'm not going to leave Adam," Cindy said firmly.

Just then the pterodactyl made another grab for Adam. He saw it coming, but it didn't help much. This time the birdlike creature used its wings as well as its claws. Adam was knocked to the ground and for a moment lost his grip on the stick. The pterodactyl was indeed smart and immediately went for the stick. It was only Watch's quick thinking that prevented them from losing their only weapon. Watch grabbed the stick before the pterodactyl could, and swung at the creature's legs, making contact. Again the pterodactyl screamed and flapped higher above them. Watch helped Adam up.

"I think I hurt it," Watch said. "Now's the time to make a run for it."

Adam nodded. "I'm game!"

They raced toward the cave they had spotted. The monster seemed prepared to let them go. It flew high into the air and appeared to search around for an easier meal. But none of them let it out of their sight. Indeed, they all had trouble running because they kept looking over their shoulders. Watch continued to hold on to the stick.

"I wish we could find another one of these," he said. "Even if we reach the cave, we won't be safe. The ptero-dactyl could always squeeze its way in."

"Maybe there'll be another stick near the cave," Adam

gasped, his shoulder still bleeding. In fact, running was making it bleed even more. He desperately needed a few minutes to stop, put pressure on the wound, and catch his breath. But he was willing to run until he bled to death. Just the thought of the pterodactyl carrying him to its nest filled him with the strength to go on.

"I have my lighter," Sally said, struggling to catch her breath with the rest of them. "If we build a fire, we could drive it off for good."

Watch glanced over his shoulder again. "It's still observing us."

"What does it want?" Cindy cried, probably more scared than any of them.

"It wants to eat us," Sally said grimly. "It will probably chew on our brains first and then begin to munch on our small intestines."

"I am so glad we have you here to tell us in what order it will eat us," Adam said.

Sally was concerned about Adam. Even as she ran, she reached over and tried to check on his wound. "You need a big bandage," she said.

"Right now I'd rather have a big shotgun," Adam replied.

The cave was only a hundred yards up ahead when the pterodactyl attacked again. They were caught off guard because the monster had momentarily disappeared over the rim of the valley through which they were running. They had taken its disappearance to mean it was leaving them. But then suddenly it appeared in front of them. Even though they all saw it, it was flying so fast that Watch didn't have time to bring up the stick.

Claws extended, the pterodactyl swept over Sally.

She was lifted off the ground.

The others screamed.

Sally, moving faster than she had ever moved in her life, leaned over and bit the pterodactyl's toes. The monster howled in pain and dropped Sally.

She rolled through about ten tumbles before she came to a halt.

The others ran to her.

"Are you all right?" Cindy cried as Adam and Watch helped Sally up.

"Yes," Sally said in a calm voice as she brushed off her clothes. "None of my bones are broken and my brain is uninjured." But then she began to shake visibly and had to put a hand to her mouth to stop herself from moaning. "That dinosaur tastes awful," she whispered.

Adam pointed toward the sky. "It's coming again. Watch, give me the stick. I think I know how to fight him off."

"Better you than me," Watch agreed, handing over the stick. "We'll keep heading for the cave."

But they weren't given a chance to head anywhere. The pterodactyl was obviously mad that his dinner had got away again. It attacked again once more, using its wings as its weapon. Adam swung at it with the stick while the others began to pelt it with rocks but the thing was simply too big and too fast to be stopped by such a defense. Plus the sound coming out of its toothy mouth was terrifying. It kept squawking as if they didn't quit fighting back and hand over one of them to eat, it would eat them all.

Then an amazing thing happened.

Watch managed to throw a rock so perfectly that it went *down* the pterodactyl's throat. There was no mistaking what happened next. The creature began to choke. Indeed, its struggle for air was so intense that it had to stop flapping its wings and land.

"This is our chance!" Adam cried. "Head for the cave!"

They took off for the dark opening.

Behind them the pterodactyl continued to gag.

The interior of the cave was dark and cool. It was a shame the opening wasn't narrow, to keep out large monsters. Watch believed it was wide enough to allow the pterodactyl inside, and for that reason they needed a fire. If they had learned one thing about the pterodactyl, they knew it didn't give up easily.

"But we've got nothing in here that will burn," Sally complained as she searched the dusty floor of the cave.

"That's not true," Watch said. "We've got the stick and we've got our clothes. If we wrap pieces of cloth around the stick we might be able to discourage the pterodactyl so that it leaves us alone."

Adam began to pull off his shirt. "Good idea. Take mine."

Sally shook her head. "Yours is too bloody. Watch, give me your shirt." Sally pulled out her Bic lighter, which she always carried no matter what. Watch quickly pulled off his shirt and the two of them began to tie it to the stick while Adam held on to the branch. Cindy was by the door of the cave, watching the pterodactyl.

"Hurry!" Cindy yelled. "It's coughed up the rock!"

The pterodactyl had recovered. But rather than fly toward the cave, it slowly began to walk in their direction. Perhaps it thought it had them cornered. The sight of the bird monster walking was even more disturbing than its flying and swooping in for an attack. Cindy began to freak out.

"We're trapped in here!" she cried.

"We're not trapped," Sally said as she touched the flame of the lighter to Watch's shirt. "But this shirt isn't going to burn very long. Cindy, give me your blouse."

Cindy stopped freaking out and looked embarrassed. "No. You burn your blouse first."

"My blouse is brand-new and cost twenty dollars for your information!" Sally snapped. "Besides, I am by nature more shy than you."

"I think the dinosaur is more shy than you," Cindy said.

"Give me the stupid stick and quit arguing!" Adam said as Watch's shirt began to catch fire. "I've got to scare it away!"

Adam pulled the stick away from Sally and hurried toward the cave entrance. He was just in time to meet the pterodactyl head on. To Adam's relief the monster recoiled from the flames. But once again Adam was struck by how smart the creature was. It seemed to know that the shirt could not burn long before going out. It withdrew several paces but didn't fly away. Beside Adam, Cindy began to panic again.

"It's not fooled!" she moaned.

Adam was grim. "It doesn't matter how many clothes we burn. It'll wait for us."

Watch moved up beside them. "I've checked, this cave doesn't go back too far. It doesn't even narrow."

Sally also joined them. "What if we draw straws or something?"

Cindy was horrified. "You mean sacrifice one of us so the others can get away?"

Sally shrugged. "I think it will be better that it doesn't get us all. While the thing is eating one of us, the other three can get away."

"Would you stop talking about its eating us!" Cindy screamed.

"Well, it ain't going to play catch with us!" Sally screamed back. "We have to face facts!"

"We're not sacrificing anybody!" Adam snapped, still holding the burning stick. "We need to come up with a better defense. Watch, you always have good ideas. Can you think of anything?"

Watch sighed. "No. And I've been racking my brain. There might be a dozen things that could drive it off, but unfortunately they're all back in town." He paused. "Let me take the stick. I'll try to keep it occupied while you guys try to make it to town."

Adam shook his head. "No way. You wouldn't last long."

"You offered to do it," Watch said.

"That was just to give you time to make it to the cave," Adam said. "How about if we try for another cave? A tighter one that the pterodactyl can't fit into?"

Watch shook his head. "I know this area better than you, and I can't think of another cave that's even close."

The flames from Watch's shirt began to flicker.

The pterodactyl took a step closer, saliva dripping out of its mouth.

"It's going out!" Cindy cried.

Adam felt desperate. "Is there any way we can block off the entrance of the cave?"

"With what?" Sally demanded. "Our dead bodies?"

"We are not going to die," Adam snapped at her. "Sally, Cindy—you two get to the rear of the cave. Watch and I will try to hold it off with the stick."

Neither of the girls protested. The sight of the pterodactyl slowly approaching on its long nailed feet was enough to shatter the strongest will. Even Adam and Watch began to back up, without consciously realizing it. The pterodactyl's huge eyes seemed to swell in anticipation. It knew it had them, that there was no escape for the frail humans.

"If only this stick was sharp at one end," Adam said bitterly. "We could stab it, make it think twice about attacking again."

"We don't have time to sharpen it," Watch said quietly.

Adam glanced over at him. "Is this it? Is this the end?"

Watch took a deep breath. "Maybe not for all of us. But it will take one of us, that's for sure."

"And that one will die?"

"Yes. Horribly."

Adam grimaced. "It can't be one of the girls."

"It can't be one of us." Watch paused. "You are brave, Adam. But even you cannot just walk in front of that beast and let it take you. No one could."

The pterodactyl skipped toward them.

The flames at the end of the stick died.

The pterodactyl stuck its head in the mouth of the cave and screeched.

"Stop it!" Cindy screamed behind them.

Adam swung weakly with the stick. "It can't get any worse than this," he gasped.

Watch put a reassuring hand on Adam's uninjured shoulder. "But this might be the perfect chance to get a good shot at it. Maybe if you went for one of its eyes, partially blind it. That could be our only hope. Aim for an eye."

Adam nodded. "I'll try."

He did try, but his effort proved useless. The pterodactyl was too quick for him, and the beast knew instinctively how to protect its eyes. It held its head back as it advanced, using its claws to lead its attack.

Several times Adam almost had his stick ripped from his hands.

Each step backward brought Adam and Watch closer to the rear of the cave, to the girls, and to the end of the line. In all the bizarre dangers Adam had faced since moving to Spooksville, he had never felt so helpless.

"I have an idea," Sally said behind Adam as he neared the rear wall. "Let's wrap another piece of cloth around the stick, set it on fire, and then crack open my lighter and douse it with what fluid is left in the container. That will create one huge flame that should last a few seconds. While it's burning, Adam, try to get the end of the stick into the thing's mouth. If that doesn't chase it away, we might be able to slip past the beast to get outside."

"We'll be easy pickings outside," Watch said. "Especially with no stick to protect us."

The pterodactyl raised a claw and swiped at them.

Adam and Watch jumped all the way back.

The four of them pushed up against the back wall of the cave.

"We are practically dessert in here!" Sally shouted. "Let's do it! Rip off the dry part of your shirt, Adam! Now!"

Adam did as he was told. In seconds Sally had the cloth wrapped around the end of the stick. First she lit the cloth and then cracked open the lighter by smashing the top of it against the cave wall. Adam had to hold the tip of the burning stick close to her, and as a result the pterodactyl was free to approach within ten feet. Sally held the open lighter fluid container not far from the burning cloth.

"When I throw this liquid on the end," she said, "there will be a burst of fire. But you'll have to move fast, Adam. Understood?"

"I understand," Adam said. "But we have to be clear about what we're doing. If we're just trying to get outside, then we'll be lucky to create a crack where we can slip by the beast. We will have to go one at a time, in order. Cindy, you go first. Then Sally and Watch. I'll follow you guys out."

"That's okay with me," Sally said eagerly, nervously eyeing the pterodactyl. "Let's do this on the count of three. One . . . Two . . . Three!"

Sally threw the fluid on the fire.

The end of the stick exploded in flames.

Adam thrust the stick at the pterodactyl just as the creature leaned forward to take a bite out of one of them. The pterodactyl had its mouth open. Adam got the end of the stick past its teeth and tongue and partway down its throat. The pterodactyl let out a deafening screech of pain and bent its narrow beak down as it tried to be rid of the fire. The stick just flew out of Adam's hands. He didn't even have a chance to react.

But the uproar created the opening they needed to get outside.

Cindy shoved by Sally and dashed past the creature. Sally followed closely, with Watch and Adam bringing up the rear. Within five seconds of attacking the pterodactyl they were back outside in the fresh air. For a moment they all felt incredible relief. But then the monster screamed from the depths of the cave and they understood that it was far from defeated.

"Run!" Adam shouted.

"Where?" Sally shouted back.

"Anywhere!" Watch said.

So they ran, back the way they had come, back up to the bluff where they had first seen the pterodactyl. But the exercise was no solution. They were dealing with an enemy that was twenty times bigger and stronger than they were. One that was used to killing to live. Really, it had been hopeless from the start.

They were almost to the bluff that overlooked Spooksville and the ocean when the pterodactyl appeared in the sky once more. It rose directly above them, higher and higher, and for a few seconds it seemed that it would keep going into the wild blue yonder and they would be safe. But then it began to arc downward, tucking in its massive wings and pointing its ugly head toward the ground. Once more it raced toward them like a deadly missile, a blur of brown death. And all the while it screeched, a horrible sound of revenge. They had hurt it and now it wanted to hurt them.

They could only stand, frozen, and watch it come.

There was only one question in their minds.

Which one of them would it take?

At the last instant the pterodactyl spread its huge wings.

A wave of foul odor and sweeping air passed over them, as well as a dark shadow. Cindy screamed, maybe they all did. But it was Cindy who screamed the loudest because the pterodactyl had chosen her to be its victim. One moment she was standing beside Adam and staring at the horror in the sky. The next she was being dragged kicking and screaming into the air. Now she was a part of the horror, and as the pterodactyl flew off to the distant peaks, it seemed as if they could hear her screaming still. Yet they all knew that was impossible.

Adam bowed his head. They all did.

Their friend was gone.

2

FOR A LONG TIME THEY REMAINED ROOTED in shock. An oppressive weight hung over them, and it seemed as if even the sun had dimmed. There were no words to express how they felt, so they said nothing. But after a while they did begin to stir.

"Could she be alive?" Sally whispered.

Watch shrugged weakly. "She could be alive at this moment."

The implications were clear. Even if she were alive now, she wouldn't be for long.

"What are we going to do?" Sally muttered.

Watch shook his head. "What can we do?"

Sally reached out and gently touched Adam's bleeding shoulder.

"We have to get you to a doctor," she said.

Adam brushed off her hand. "I'm not going to a doctor."

Watch glanced at him. "You can't go after her."

Adam stared hard at him. "I'm not just going to leave her to the whim of that creature."

"It's hopeless," Sally said.

Adam screamed at her. "It's not hopeless! You just don't want to try to save her because you don't like her!"

Sally had tears on her face. "I would do anything to save her, if I thought there was one chance in a million. But there is no chance, Adam."

Adam paused and lowered his head. "I didn't mean that. I know she was your friend, too. I'm sorry I yelled at you."

Sally squeezed his arm. "That's all right. We all know how much you liked Cindy."

Watch cleared his throat. "Let's not bury her just yet. I've been thinking some more, and there is a chance she's alive, and may be alive for a while longer, long enough to be rescued maybe."

Adam raised his eyes. "What do you mean? That pterodactyl looked starving."

Watch stared at the mountain peaks where Cindy had disappeared. "We assume the pterodactyl was hunting for itself, that it was hungry. But none of us knows what a hungry pterodactyl looks like. What if the creature was actually hunting for its babies?"

"You think that was a mama pterodactyl?" Sally asked.

"There's a good chance it was," Watch said. "And if it brought Cindy back to its nest to feed its young, it might not kill her right away. Most reptiles like to eat living things."

"But the children will be waiting hungrily," Sally said in a shaky voice.

"Not necessarily," Watch said. "The mother obviously hunts in the daytime, and maybe even at night. But I read an article once that postulated that most baby dinosaurs slept away the majority of the day. And it's an especially hot day today. They might all be asleep when the pterodactyl returns to its nest with Cindy."

Adam's face suddenly regained life. "Then we have to go after them now!"

Watch stopped him. "We can't go after Cindy or the pterodactyl on foot, at least not for the first part of the trip. Those mountaintops are miles away. We need to

25

get a car or, better yet, a four-wheel-drive truck. There's a road up into those mountains that I know." He paused. "We'll head toward town, find some transportation, and I'll go after her."

"Why you?" Adam asked.

Watch listed the reasons. "Because I know how to drive. Because I know those mountains. Because you're injured. Because you're both forgetting something important—where there is one dinosaur, there can be two dinosaurs. You two have to get back to town and warn everyone what's happening."

"It's true that Adam is injured and should stay behind," Sally said. "But I should go with you, Watch."

Watch shook his head. "It's too dangerous. Why risk both of us? Two of us won't improve Cindy's chances of survival. Also, you two will work better if you're together. And I think better alone."

"What are we working on?" Adam asked, feeling weak from the loss of blood and the grief. He still could not believe Cindy was gone. He kept expecting to look over and see her smiling face. The sound of her screams as the creature dragged her away haunted him.

"Isn't it obvious?" Watch said. "We have to figure out what dinosaurs are doing in our time, in our city. Then we have to discover a way to get rid of them."

"Do you have any theories?" Sally asked.

Watch nodded. "I have a basic theory. Somehow our time must have merged with an ancient time. There haven't been pterodactyls on earth in seventy million years. But what caused this merger I have no idea."

"Do you think the two times are just merging here, or all over the world?" Adam asked.

"I hope just here," Watch said. "If our time and the time of the dinosaurs have merged everywhere, we're in real trouble. But I don't think that's the case. We have seen only one pterodactyl, not dozens. The doorway between the two times is probably localized."

"But what could open such a doorway?" Sally asked.

"I have no idea," Watch answered simply.

"Even if the gap between the times is localized, it must be big," Adam said, "for these creatures to get through it. What if it's several miles across?"

"It's all relative," Watch said. "If we can figure out how to close it, we can close it. Otherwise it doesn't matter how big or small it is. Also, my theory might be way off. Maybe the pterodactyl came from some strange place, not some other time."

They started back to town. Adam soon began to feel so weak he needed to lean on Watch for support. Sally tore up what was left of Adam's shirt and made it into a bandage of sorts. Finally Adam's bleeding stopped but he continued to feel drained.

Sally wept quietly as they walked. They hoped to rescue Cindy. They would do everything they could to save her. But they weren't fooling themselves. The pterodactyl had been a fierce enemy. Cindy was probably dead already.

When they were about a quarter of a mile outside of town, they came across a parked truck. It was an odd place to find a truck. But it met Watch's highest criteria. It was a four-wheel-drive vehicle with a powerful engine and huge wheels. The body of the blue truck was jacked up so high they could almost walk under it. The only problem was that it was locked, and there were no keys.

"I know how to hot-wire a truck," Watch said, picking up a rock.

"That's stealing," Sally said. Then she added, "But who cares at a time like this?"

Adam nodded. "Break the window and get going, Watch. Sally and I can make it back to town."

Watch smashed the window with the rock. The sound made them all jump. "Maybe I should drive you back," Watch said as he reached inside and unlocked the door. "It'll take only a few minutes."

"No," Adam said. "A few minutes might be the difference between life and death for Cindy." He momentarily leaned on the truck for support. "You'll need a miracle to find the pterodactyl's nest."

Watch brushed the glass off the front seat and climbed inside. "Not necessarily. I should be able to hear its screeching miles away."

"But I bet the nest will be up high," Sally said. "You're going to have to do some hiking. And then the pterodactyl will probably attack you once you're out of the truck."

Watch smashed the ignition with his stone and pulled out the exposed wires. "Before it gets to me, you can be sure I'll have a big stick," Watch said. After touching the ends of a black and red wire together, Watch heard the engine turn over and start. It roared to life as Watch pressed the gas. He added, "I think this truck will take me pretty close to where I need to go."

Sally reached up and hugged Watch. "Don't take any unnecessary risks. Always try to know where you can take shelter. And keep your eyes and ears open at all times."

Watch nodded. "I'll be careful."

Adam squeezed Watch's arm. "Good luck. If you're able to save her, you'll be the biggest hero in the world. At least you'll be our hero."

Watch also squeezed Adam's hand and looked him straight in the eye. "I don't think she's dead," he said seriously. "If she was, we would feel it, you know? I don't feel it."

Adam nodded sadly. "Let's hope for the best."

Watch shut the door and gunned the engine, and soon the truck was just a cloud of settling dust on the narrow road that led up into the mountains. Adam and Sally watched it disappear with heavy hearts.

"Should we have let him go?" she asked.

Adam sighed. "Did we have a choice?"

"I hope the pterodactyl doesn't get him, too."

"I hope it doesn't get all of us," Adam said.

With that they turned once again toward town.

They had been walking less than two minutes when they realized they weren't alone. They had another visitor. Its head poked up over the surrounding trees. This one was bigger than the pterodactyl—unquestionably a real dinosaur.

And there was a kid riding on its back.

3

WHEN CINDY FIRST WOKE UP SHE FELT AND knew nothing except a pounding in her head. The stabs of pain came in rhythm, as if her blood were performing an insane dance on top of her delicate nerve endings. She moaned and the sound seemed to come from far away.

It was only slowly that she became aware of her surroundings and remembered what had happened to her on the bluff. Although her friends had heard her scream all the way back into the mountains, Cindy had really been unconscious during the deadly flight. Her mouth had been screaming, not her mind. She had either gone into shock or been knocked out almost as soon as the pterodactyl grabbed her.

But the horror of that attack came back to her now and she sat up quickly and opened her eyes, stunned by what she saw.

She was in a nest so huge it could have housed a thousand normal birds. It was pieced together out of branches, mud, even a couple whole logs. It stunk of decomposing vegetation, and she had to hold her nose to keep from being sick. The nest had been built into a rocky crevasse near the top of a peak that didn't look even vaguely familiar. Peering over the edge, Cindy didn't even recognize the *type* of trees and bushes that lay far below. Even the sky was a strange color, purple streaked with heavy gray, that glittered with distant lightning.

Then there were the eggs. They lay off to her right, four of them, leaning against one another for support. Each was almost as big as Cindy and sickly yellow in color. As she stared at them the egg closest to her began to crack on the top.

"That's just great," Cindy said. "Now I'm going to be baby food."

Fortunately the mother pterodactyl was nowhere to be seen, and Cindy believed she could handle a single baby dinosaur. But she worried that all four might hatch at once, and she shuddered to think of the babies surrounding her and pecking at her flesh. Also, the mother could return at any moment and seriously wound her so that she couldn't put up a fight. Cindy realized that her blacking out was probably the only thing that had saved her. The mother pterodactyl had probably thought that she would be an easy meal for her children.

The top of the egg broke open and a single tiny claw emerged.

The creature inside screeched thinly.

Cindy knew she had to get out of the nest.

But the mother pterodactyl had built wisely, so close to the edge of the rocky peak that only the most agile enemies could prey on the eggs. Standing up, Cindy decided that her only chance was to climb up to the top of the peak, and hope there was a way down the other side. On this side there was nothing but sheer cliff below her.

Cindy was gripping the side of the nest when the first baby pterodactyl spilled out of its crumbling egg. The creature had simple needs. It was alive and now it wanted to eat. The first thing it did was stagger free of the ghostly fluid that covered its pale brown body. Then it screeched at Cindy.

"Food!" it seemed to say. Cindy tried to pull herself out of the nest but was forced to stop to defend herself.

The pterodactyl wanted a bite of her leg. Cindy watched in horror as it scampered toward her.

"Leave me alone!" Cindy cried, kicking at it, which gave it reason to pause but not go away. Cindy tried not to think about what would have happened if she hadn't regained consciousness a few minutes earlier. The baby pterodactyl would have just walked over and begun to feed on her. Like Sally said, it probably would have fed on her brain first.

Yuck!

Cindy kicked at it again and the nasty little baby had the nerve to scratch her right leg with one of its claws. Cindy couldn't believe how painful the cut was, and wondered if baby pterodactyls had poison on the tips of their claws. But the weird thing was she didn't really want to hurt the creature, even though it was trying to eat her. She understood that attacking any living thing was its nature, that it was just hungry. At the same time she wasn't feeling warm enough toward the creature to take it home and build it a playhouse.

But where was home?

These couldn't be the mountains that surrounded Spooksville.

The shape of them, the plants that grew on them—everything looked primeval. It was as if the mother pterodactyl had not merely carried her away, but carried her into the past—far into the past.

Of course it was the present moment she was worried about.

The baby pterodactyl tried to scratch her again and Cindy was forced to kick it. She caught it with a clean shot and the little monster howled and backed off.

"Let that be a lesson to you," Cindy said. "Don't go trying to eat things that are bigger than you."

Cindy managed to pull herself out of the nest and onto a narrow ledge that ran along the mountain peak. But the drop below her was at least two thousand feet. Her head spun. Desperately she clutched the surrounding stone. She had always been afraid of heights. Even riding up in an elevator in a tall building could make her dizzy. Trying not to look down, she slowly made her way toward a sharp break in the wall of the cliff that offered her handholds to pull herself up to the top of the peak. Behind her, the baby pterodactyl continued to screech. Cindy hoped it wasn't calling for mom to come home quick.

But that was probably exactly what it was doing.

Cindy carefully began to pull herself up, making sure with each step that her weight was fully supported. She wasn't far from the top of the mountain, maybe only two hundred feet. But that two hundred feet took her ages to cover. Glancing down set her head spinning, yet the temptation to do so refused to leave her. For the time being, she was her own worst enemy. She kept telling herself to stay cool, that she was lucky to be alive.

After what seemed an hour of climbing she pulled herself up on top of the peak. For a moment the view stole her breath away. In every direction was the most exotic scenery she had ever seen. Massive waterfalls plunging thousands of feet into churning pools. Purple colored trees, larger than redwoods, that seemed to be straining to touch the sky with fat branches covered in blue leaves.

There was even a volcano, blowing off dirty steam, percolating off to the far side of the peak. It looked like a classic volcano, cone shaped, with black sides and an angrily glowing red tip. But just the sight of it made Cindy uneasy. Maybe it had been shooting off steam for ages, but there was something immediately threatening about it. Was it ready to blow its top?

"This is definitely not Spooksville," she said out loud to herself.

But then where was she?

She wasn't given a chance to think about the question. A terrifying sound—like the huge beating heart

Watch had described—could be heard in the distance. Cindy strained her eyes in every direction but didn't see anything. The sky was largely covered with thick gray clouds, and she knew her old friend the pterodactyl had to be hiding behind them. The pulsing sound grew louder and louder. When the monster finally emerged it was less than a hundred yards away. Cindy started to scream. Clearly it must have come for her, and standing on top of the peak she was totally exposed and completely helpless. Yet the pterodactyl swept past her as if she didn't exist, aiming at something or someone far below her. Curious, Cindy crept to the far edge and looked down. She could see nothing, but was amazed she could hear something.

A human voice. A friend calling to her?

"IS THAT AN APATOSAURUS?" ADAM ASKED as the kid on top came into view.

"Is that Bryce Poole?" Sally asked, showing what was more important to her.

The answer to both questions was of course "yes." Who else would be riding a dinosaur into town but the dark and handsome Bryce Poole? At least Sally might have posed the question that way. For his part, Adam was more interested in the dinosaur. It had to be about ninety feet long and weigh over thirty tons. It shook the ground as it moved. Bryce waved to them as the dinosaur swung its small gray head in their direction.

"Don't worry!" Bryce called. "This one is a vegetarian."

"We know that!" Adam yelled back. "But what are you doing with that dinosaur?"

"Isn't it obvious?" Bryce yelled back. "I am riding it into town. I need to show everyone that we're in real danger."

Sally gushed to Adam. "Isn't it incredible that he could tame a real live dinosaur?"

Adam frowned. "I don't think he's tamed anything. That dinosaur looks like its going where it wants when it wants."

"Oh, you're just jealous," Sally huffed. Then she smiled and waved brightly to Bryce. "Why don't you come down here and talk to us? We need your help."

"We don't need his help," Adam muttered, thinking of the time Bryce Poole had helped them when they were trapped in the Dark Corner on the other side of the Secret Path. Bryce had run off as soon as they showed up. He left them to fend for themselves against the demons. For that reason, neither Adam nor Watch trusted Bryce. But the girls couldn't get enough of him, much to Adam's dismay.

"I'll be down in a few seconds!" Bryce called back. And with that he said a few words to the apatosaurus and, by golly, if the massive beast didn't lower its head and neck so that Bryce could slide off. He casually strolled up to them. "What's happening?" he asked.

"For your information we were just attacked by a

pterodactyl," Adam said. "Cindy was carried away, and Watch has gone to rescue her."

"I know," Bryce said. "I saw the whole thing as I was riding down from the mountains."

Adam was angry. "Then why didn't you help us?"

Sally interrupted. "Obviously Bryce would have helped us if he had had a chance. He must have been too far away. Isn't that right, Bryce?"

"Yes," Bryce said. "I was riding the apatosaurus, but you can't make it go faster." He paused. "I really hope Watch is able to rescue Cindy. I know if I had been there she would probably be safe now."

"I don't think so," Adam said, amazed that Bryce could say such a thing with a straight face.

"Adam has been through a rough time," Sally told Bryce. "You have to forgive his bad manners."

Adam rolled his eyes. "I'm the one who needs to be forgiven. You still haven't explained what you're doing with that dinosaur."

"Yes, I have," Bryce said. "I am taking it into town. We have to mobilize against this invasion."

"What are the dinosaurs doing here?" Sally asked.

"An interdimensional time warp has opened between present time and seventy million years ago," Bryce explained. "The warp is way back in the mountains."

"Watch figured that out already," Adam said.

Bryce shook his head. "What Watch couldn't know is what he will find on the other side of the mountains. A doorway hasn't simply opened to the past. Actual pieces of the past have materialized here and covered the land just beyond Spooksville. What I'm saying is we have mountains and volcanoes from seventy million years ago sitting just beyond those peaks."

"So you've been there?" Sally asked, impressed.

Bryce was grim. "Yes. I've been studying this phenomena for the last two days, and have been trying to find a solution to it. But so far I haven't been able to stop it."

"But I know you will," Sally said with stars in her eyes.

"If you knew about these dinosaurs two days ago," Adam complained, "you were awfully slow in warning people."

"I didn't want to start a panic," Bryce said.

Adam was bitter. "A panic? We had a little panic this morning when a pterodactyl carried Cindy away. If you hadn't decided to try to solve this problem all by yourself, she would probably be here now."

Bryce nodded reluctantly. "I may have made a mistake. But I did accomplish a great deal in the last two days, even if I haven't reversed the time warp. I do know that we can use the Secret Path to help stop it."

"How do you know that?" Adam snapped.

"The Secret Path is not just a path into other dimensions. It is also a portal into other times. I am convinced that what created this time warp exists in the past."

Adam snickered. "You're just guessing. You don't know any more than we do."

"You're wrong," Bryce said simply. "About this phenomena I know a great deal more than any of you, and that includes Watch. For example, I know that for time to have become so distorted a tremendous amount of energy must have been set loose in the past, probably seventy million years ago. I also know that this explosion—if you want to call it that—must have happened at a place that was susceptible to time as well as space fractures."

"I don't know what you're talking about," Adam said. He really didn't.

Bryce spoke with patience. "Madeline Templeton's tombstone in the Spooksville cemetery is the one place that leads to the Secret Path. It is a natural spot for space and time distortion. It's my belief that the explosion that occurred in the past happened there. It sent a ripple of time space distortion into our time and space."

"But you say land from seventy million years ago lies beyond the mountains," Adam protested. "The cemetery is on this side of the mountains. I don't see the connection."

"The doorway to the Secret Path is here now," Bryce said. "But where was it seventy million years ago? Whole continents have shifted since then. I think in the past the cemetery and what is happening on the other side of the mountains overlapped. I'm going to use the Secret Path to go back in time to stop the explosion from ever happening."

"What a magnificent plan!" Sally exclaimed.

"And you just thought you'd ride a dinosaur into town while you were at it?" Adam muttered, still annoyed at Bryce's nerve. Yet despite himself, Adam was impressed by Bryce's logic.

Bryce spoke darkly. "I may fail in my plan, and die in the past. I told you twice why I am riding this dinosaur. Why don't you believe me?"

"Adam suffers from poor self-esteem," Sally explained. "His nasty remarks are just part of a defense mechanism."

"I believe you," Adam said reluctantly. "But I suspect you won't need to ride a dinosaur to warn people of the danger. I think a few dinosaurs will get there ahead of us, at least as long as we waste time by standing here arguing. Also, I still think it's a mistake to tackle this problem all by yourself. We could help."

"I just don't want to expose you to danger," Bryce said. "If something happened to you, I'd never be able to forgive myself."

"I'd forgive you," Sally said quickly.

Adam frowned some more. "Ann Templeton knows more about the Secret Path than any of us, and she is a powerful witch. Since all of Spooksville is in danger, I say we head to her castle first to try to get her help."

"That will slow us down," Bryce warned.

"Not much," Adam replied. "Her castle and the cemetery are right next to each other." Adam added, "You can't be so sure of yourself that you don't need help."

"Some heroes work better alone," Sally said.

Bryce nodded. "I don't mind help. I'm not an egomaniac, no matter what you think, Adam. I just don't want to see any more people killed."

"Cindy could be alive," Adam said flatly. "We haven't given up on her."

"I understand." Bryce turned back toward the apatosaurus, which appeared to be waiting for him. "Let's all ride Sara back to town."

Sally hurried to catch up with Bryce. "Did you name her after me? You know my real name is Sara Wilcox."

Bryce shrugged. "Maybe subconsciously."

"Oh brother," Adam muttered.

5

WATCH WAS SURPRISED WHEN THE ROAD
ran out and he entered a primeval forest. He realized
immediately that he had to revamp his theory about
a doorway to the past opening. The doorway had not
only opened, the past had at least pushed a portion of
itself through.

He was fortunate, however, that he was able to
keep driving even without the road. For a while the ter-
rain remained relatively flat. But he could see the sharp
peaks in the distance getting closer with each passing
minute. He suspected that was where the pterodactyl had taken Cindy and he tried to take the truck as
close as he could. But soon enough he was on foot and

climbing. There were six peaks to chose from—he just chose the closest one.

He had been climbing less than thirty minutes when he saw and heard two things almost simultaneously. He caught a peek at what looked like a huge nest partway around the steep peak he was scaling. Above that, in the low hanging clouds, he heard the strange beating sound he associated with the attack of the pterodactyl. He was therefore not surprised when the monster suddenly pierced through the clouds and dove in his direction.

But he was surprised, and relieved, to see Cindy appear at the top of the peak.

He waved. "Cindy!" he shouted.

She waved back. "Watch! Be careful!"

The pterodactyl was coming. Maybe it remembered him from the cave. The screech that rang out from its long mouth certainly didn't sound friendly. For a moment Watch was utterly perplexed as to what to do. A quick glance around revealed there were no sticks handy. But what he did have were some places to take shelter. The trouble with hiding, though, was that he would leave Cindy open to attack. From what he could see she was completely exposed on the peak. No, he thought, he had to hurt the pterodactyl, and he had to hurt it bad.

The pterodactyl screamed. It would be on him in seconds.

There was a cave directly off to Watch's left. Yet it was no ordinary cave. It seemed to form a loop in the side of the cliff. In other words, he could walk in one entrance and walk out a hundred feet higher up. It got Watch thinking that if he could entice the pterodactyl to come after him on the lower level, he could slip up and around and try to attack it from above.

Of course he didn't know *what* he would attack it with.

Now he wished he had taken time to go to town for a gun.

Watch waved his arm at the approaching creature.

"Here I am!" he shouted. "Come get me!"

"Don't do that!" Cindy screamed from far above. "Take cover!"

Watch inched closer to the shelter, but waited till the last possible second to rush into the cave. He almost waited too long. He actually felt the brush of the pterodactyl's wings as he slipped into the hole in the cliff wall. He was lucky the monster paused once it landed and took a moment to get its bearings. During that time Watch managed to work his way through the cave to come out the other end one hundred feet above the creature. To his immense pleasure he found a large boulder sitting at the opening to the cave. Now if he could just roll it off the edge and onto the head of the pterodactyl, the day could be saved.

The only problem was when he looked down the pterodactyl had disappeared.

It had slipped into the cave.

Watch whirled around, half expecting to find the monster preparing to jump on his back. What he did see was terrifying enough. The pterodactyl had followed him into the cave and had even climbed up the same way he had. The only problem—as far as the hungry pterodactyl was concerned—was that the cave narrowed at the top. Narrowed too much for a full-grown flying lizard to squeeze past. The monster could see Watch and he could see it but it couldn't get him. Watch almost laughed out loud.

"It's your turn to feel what it's like to be trapped," Watch said as he knelt to pick up a rock. Yet the pterodactyl was not necessarily trapped. It could probably back up. Watch wanted it to back up and wander down to the lower level so he could roll the boulder on top of it.

That is why Watch began to throw rocks at its head.

The pterodactyl didn't like that. Its screeches turned loud and bitter.

"Watch!" Cindy cried from far above.

"I've got it where I want it!" Watch yelled back to her.

And a few minutes later he did indeed have it where he wanted it.

The pterodactyl finally got annoyed being pelted with rocks and crawled back down the tunnel. It reemerged a minute later directly below Watch. Watch was waiting for it—he knew he had to act quickly. The moment the pterodactyl raised its head to look up at him, he gave the boulder a hard shove. The position of his prey couldn't have been better.

The pterodactyl let out a yelp as the big rock crashed down on its head.

For a moment Watch thought he had killed it and felt inexplicably bad. The pterodactyl, after all, had been trying to kill them for half the day. But then he realized that the creature was still alive, only knocked unconscious. The boulder had rolled to the side and he could see that the creature was still breathing, although it was bleeding slightly from the side of its ugly head. Watch figured it would be up and hungry soon. He had to get out of this place as quick as possible.

Yet as Watch hiked up to where Cindy was waiting for him, he continually glanced at the nearby volcano. From the amount of red-lit steam it was bellowing, it appeared to be on the verge of rupturing. That made him wonder if the volcano had something to do with the time warp. Because Watch did understand—despite what Mr.-Know-It-All-Bryce-Poole had said to Adam— that time and energy and space were directly connected. In fact, before Watch reached Cindy, he had changed his mind. He didn't want to leave this primeval time, after all. At least not until he understood more about what had brought it into the present. He was willing to risk the obvious dangers of these weird forests and mountains to get to the truth.

He could only imagine what Cindy would have to say about that.

6

WHEN ADAM, SALLY, AND BRYCE REACHED
Ann Templeton's castle, they were horrified to find
it under attack by a forty-foot tyrannosaurus. The
most famous of all dinosaurs—and certainly the most
feared—was immersed in the waters of the witch's
fabled moat. Seeing the monster, Sara, their obedient
apatosaurus, quickly turned and tried to run away. But
somehow Bryce managed to convince it to let them
off before it headed for safer ground. Fortunately the
tyrannosaurus saw neither Sara nor them. Together,
the three of them huddled behind some bushes and
watched as the tyrannosaurus took on Spooksville's
most powerful citizen.

"Still want to go to the witch for help?" Bryce asked Adam.

"I think Ann Templeton can handle this creature," Adam said calmly, although he was far from sure. The roar of the tyrannosaurus made the screech of the pterodactyl sound almost welcoming. The alligators and crocodiles in the moat were all attacking the tyrannosaurus but they were mere annoyances to the dinosaur. It only had to step on them as they got near, and they were history. The tyrannosaurus seemed serious about getting into the castle. It was dismantling the structure brick by brick. To Adam's amazement, Sally seemed to take pleasure in the battle.

"I think this time she is going to get her backside whipped," she said hopefully.

Adam was disgusted. "How can you be rooting for the dinosaur? Ann Templeton has never done anything to you."

"Have you forgotten that she locked us in her castle and tortured us?" Sally asked.

"She didn't torture us," Adam said impatiently. "She just made sure we had an adventure is all."

"Yeah. Getting attacked by her poisonous spiders was tons of fun," Sally said.

"Look!" Bryce pointed. "She's sending out her trolls."

It was true—a small squadron of trolls had appeared

at the top of the castle. They were armed with spears and long bows. Yet their arrows, as they landed on the thick hide of the tyrannosaurus, served only to anger the giant beast. With its massive head and seven-inch teeth it reached up and grabbed a troll in its mouth. The poor guy didn't have a chance. Even as he started to scream, he was ground to pieces. He was swallowed with his legs still kicking. Sally turned her head away in horror.

"You're right," she whispered. "I can't cheer for this monster."

The tyrannosaurus snatched up a few more trolls before they could retreat inside the castle with the rest. These other victims were also chewed down, and their cries chilled Adam's blood. He couldn't stop thinking about Cindy.

"I think the witch has met her match," Bryce said quietly.

"It ain't over till it's over," Adam said without much hope. The tyrannosaurus returned to tearing down the thick castle walls. But then, a tongue of green flame suddenly leapt out from the highest castle tower. Adam just caught a glimpse of Ann Templeton standing above the dinosaur, wielding her mystical powers.

The power of the flame sent the tyrannosaurus into a frenzy. It responded by tearing more fiercely at the castle.

Once more Ann Templeton raised her arm. A second bolt of flame leapt from the tower. This one, blue in color, lashed at the seemingly impenetrable hide of the tyrannosaurus. But now the beast felt real pain, and perhaps fear. A gruesome cut now scarred its massive side. Rather than continue to attack the castle, the dinosaur plowed off in the direction of town. From far away Adam heard people screaming and tried not to think about what was happening to them. Beside him Bryce nodded with grudging respect.

"She was able to drive it off," he said. "But she can't drive off all the dinosaurs. If the doorway is to be closed that is allowing them into our world, then we must go through the Secret Path now."

"We can't go through the Secret Path without first walking all over town," Adam said.

"That's not true, I know a shortcut," Bryce said.

"What?" Adam asked.

"I am not going to tell you exactly how I do it," Bryce said. "Just follow me, if you dare, and we will travel seventy million years back in time."

"Why won't you tell me how you do it?" Adam demanded.

"Because you don't trust me, and I don't trust you," Bryce said simply. "Now come, let's get to the cemetery before the tyrannosaurus returns."

Adam hesitated. "I still want to talk to Ann Templeton."

They heard more screams in the distance.

It sounded as if people were being torn to death.

And who really knew how many tyrannosauruses there were?

Bryce stood impatiently. "How many people have to die while you talk to everyone in town?"

"He's right, Adam," Sally said. "We have to act now. Soon there won't be any Spooksville left to save."

Adam considered. "If we go back in time and fix what is causing the problem in our time, then all the deaths and injuries in our time would never have occurred. What I mean is, we should be able to fix everything in the present by correcting the past."

"Then it won't matter how many die right now?" Sally asked. "They will be alive if we succeed in the past?"

Adam paused. "It shouldn't matter. I have to talk to Ann Templeton."

Bryce gave him a penetrating look and nodded. "Your theory sounds logical, Adam, and it might be true. But are you willing to risk Cindy's life—and the lives of everyone else in town—for a theory?"

It was the million-dollar question.

And Adam wasn't sure how to answer it.

7

As Watch and Cindy hiked toward the volcano, Cindy didn't try to stop Watch from exploring more as he had worried she might. She was just so grateful to him for coming to rescue her that she said he could do whatever he wanted and she would stay by his side. Watch thought Cindy was a great girl, as far as girls went. In reality Watch was still getting used to girls. They were not like boys, no.

As they drew closer to the volcano, Watch realized he had been seeing something without consciously noticing it. The volcano had drawn him to it, but now he understood that a part of his brain must have realized what that shiny spot near the base of the volcano really was. He either had to get better glasses or else he had to listen to his own intuition more.

There was a flying saucer parked near the base of the volcano.

It was silver and shiny, but it wasn't exactly shaped like the saucers they had seen when their friend Ekwee12 had visited them from the future. For one thing this saucer was much larger and higher relative to its width. Watch suspected it was from an entirely different race of beings, and of course Cindy wondered if they were friendly.

"I wonder what they're doing here," she said.

"I wonder what they're doing here at this time," Watch said.

Cindy caught a peculiar note in his voice. "By 'this time' are you implying that we are back in time?"

Watch shrugged. "It sure looks like it."

Cindy stopped him. "Wait. Then I'm confused. I thought this whole place came from the past and was overlaid on to our present. But that we were still in the present."

Watch removed his thick glasses and cleaned them on his pants leg. He still had no shirt. The high humidity of the area was fogging up his lenses. Putting his glasses back on again he scanned the immediate area. He was constantly on the lookout for dinosaurs.

"We may have passed through the time doorway

when we came here," he said. "Or else we may still be in the present. I'm not sure. But I don't think this ship is here by coincidence. It's got to be related to what's happening with this invasion of dinosaurs."

"You mean you think these aliens caused the rip in time?"

"It's possible. Or maybe they're here to prevent the rip in time, too."

Cindy was doubtful. "They must be behind the attack of the dinosaurs. That makes more sense."

Watch gestured toward the volcano. "We won't know until we meet them." He started once more on his way. "We don't have far to go."

They did, in fact, reach the saucer within the next half hour, but no one appeared to be at home. They shouted and even pounded on the shiny metal but no one poked his head out. There was, however, a black cave nearby, which could lead into the heart of the volcano. But just before they entered it the ground rumbled and a huge cloud of steam belched overhead. This cloud was shot through with a haunting red light, which obviously came from the hot fires percolating deep inside the volcano. Now Cindy was beginning to have second thoughts about exploring. She gestured to the cave entrance.

"It feels awfully warm in there," she said. "The volcano must be on the verge of erupting. Do you think it's a good idea to enter an erupting volcano?"

"I think it's very dangerous idea to explore a volcanic cave at any time, especially now when it may or may not be filled with aliens," Watch said. "But I also think it's just as dangerous to return to Spooksville with the mystery of the time warp unsolved. For all we know our town could be under heavy dinosaur attack at this very minute. People might be dying."

Cindy stared at the dark opening. "I have a bad feeling about this."

"You can stay outside if you want. I won't tell Sally."

Cindy smiled. "I'm not worried about Sally's opinion. Did she get upset when I got carried away by the pterodactyl?"

"She wept."

"No!"

"Really. She was distraught."

Cindy shook her head in wonder. "So all I have to do to get her to like me is to die. Isn't that weird?"

"It's the same with most people." Watch gestured to the cave. "We better get inside. I wouldn't be surprised if this volcano started dripping lava at any minute."

Cindy followed him. "If that happens we won't be able to get back outside," she warned.

The interior of the cave was not merely uncomfortably warm but intensely hot. Had the temperature been any higher their skin would have begun to blister. Also, the air was thick with sulfur fumes. They tried not to cough because they didn't want any aliens to know they were coming, but it was next to impossible to breathe normally. Cindy found herself growing dizzy and Watch's vision began to blur. Still, they kept on because they were from Spooksville and they were used to adventures and saving the world.

After about a hundred yards the cave split in three directions. It was like the Haunted Cave. They weren't sure which tunnel to take. But Cindy believed she heard voices coming from the middle one. Yet she wasn't positive. Watch couldn't hear anything.

"But we might want to come at them from the side," he said. "And observe what they're doing before we introduce ourselves."

Cindy nodded. "Why don't we take the tunnel on the right then? It might loop around and join the others."

"Sounds like a plan," Watch said.

They were in the new cave a few minutes when Cindy asked Watch, "Were you upset when the pterodactyl stole me away?"

"I came after you, didn't I?"

Cindy leaned over and gave him a hug. "Maybe you should be my boyfriend instead of Adam."

Watch was astounded. "Adam is your boyfriend?"

Cindy paused. "Well, yes, sort of."

"Does he know that?"

Cindy frowned. "Maybe he doesn't. Should I tell him?"

Watch shook his head. "No. Why break up a perfect relationship?"

The tunnel on the right eventually opened into a large underground chamber. They had no trouble seeing; the place was lit with simmering pools of lava, and alien light bulbs. The chamber was far from empty.

There were four aliens in it, all working around a metal box that was as big as an office desk. The aliens could have passed for human beings except for their long white hair and shiny silver suits. But even though their hair was white, none of them appeared to be over thirty. Indeed, they were a beautiful-looking people with clear tan skin and bright blue eyes. On the metal belts that circled their waists they carried communication devices and hand weapons. It was these pieces of technology that made Watch hesitate to talk to them. He leaned over and whispered in Cindy's ear.

"They look friendly," he said. "But they're obviously armed. Plus we don't know what that metal box is."

"You don't want to talk to them?" Cindy asked.

"I want to watch a few minutes more before deciding."

"What do you think the box could be?"

Watch shrugged. "A computer of some kind. A bomb, maybe."

Cindy gasped. "A bomb? You mean, they might be trying to set this volcano off?"

"It's possible."

"Could the eruption of this volcano be responsible for the time warp?"

Watch was doubtful. "By itself a huge explosion in the past should not affect the present. There have been big explosions all over the world throughout time. But maybe there will be something special about this explosion."

"What?" Cindy asked.

"I don't know."

"But shouldn't we stop them if it is a bomb?"

Watch was doubtful. "It would seem so. But I'd rather wait and not do anything just yet."

"But what are we waiting for?"

"For something to happen," Watch said simply.

Something did happen a few minutes later, something dramatic. Without warning red bolts of laser fire erupted from the far side of the volcanic chamber. Two of the aliens were immediately struck down. They fell to the ground with expressions of intense pain. The other two aliens fled in the direction of the tunnel where Watch and Cindy were crouched. But these two did not go down easily. They fired back as they fled, and Watch and Cindy heard a howl of pain rise from the unseen enemy in the far cave.

Yet the two remaining aliens—the ones Watch and Cindy could see—had poor position. There was no cover in the chamber, and before they could reach the safety of the tunnel, they each took a laser blast to the chest and crumpled to the floor. There they lay on their backs with twisted expressions of pain on their faces. Their eyes were still open, however—they appeared dead. Cindy turned away in horror.

"They just murdered them," she moaned.

"Yeah," Watch whispered. The attackers had yet to show their faces, and the last of the aliens to go down had fallen not far from where Watch was crouched. But Watch feared to reach for the alien's hand laser, afraid it would expose them to attack. It was probably a wise move because less than a minute later another group of four aliens appeared.

These were also largely humanoid. Yet their heads were larger than humans, and they were completely bald. Also, their eyes were strange, more like black slits revealing empty souls than organs for seeing. They wore shiny black uniforms and moved quickly to secure the chamber, making sure that each of the four aliens was definitely down and out.

Next they turned their attention to the metal box the others had been working on. They seemed to argue briefly over what the reading on the box's instrument panel meant. Their voices were high-pitched and scratchy, and both Watch and Cindy became disturbed as they watched.

"I think they're bad," Cindy whispered.

Watch was unsure. "Why? Because they're not as handsome as the others?"

"No. You saw the way they just shot the others down without warning."

"But these two races are probably enemies. The first ones might have shot these guys down if they'd been given the chance."

Cindy shook her head. "I don't think so. I don't think any civilized race would kill without warning."

"Good point. But which one of these races is the most civilized? See, we don't know anything until we know what that metal box is, what it's here for."

"You think it may be here to cause the time warp?" Cindy asked.

"Or else stop it."

Cindy was anxious. "We have to do something!"

Watch nodded grimly. "Yeah, I know. But after seeing how these new guys just blew away the others, I don't exactly feel like walking out there and introducing myself." Watch paused. "We'll wait a few more minutes, see if the situation changes any."

A few minutes later the situation did change again. Behind Watch and Cindy, they noticed a peculiar light shimmering against one wall of the tunnel. For a moment they feared that the aliens had circled around them and were firing on them. But such was not the case because a few moments later the glowing wall momentarily dissolved and Bryce and Sally appeared. Watch and Cindy ran to them.

"What are you guys doing here?" Cindy asked.

"Cindy!" Sally exclaimed, giving her a hug. "I thought you were dead!"

"Hush!" Watch whispered. "There's a group of aliens just a few yards down this cave. They are armed and dangerous, and we can't let them know we're here."

"Thank you for worrying about me," Cindy said, patting Sally on the back. But Sally was suddenly embarrassed. She let go of Cindy and brushed her hands on her shirt.

"I wasn't that worried," she muttered.

"Tell me about these aliens," Bryce snapped at Watch.

Watch didn't blink. "First tell me how you got here?"

"We took the Secret Path," Sally said. "Bryce knows how to use it to move through time. Adam decided to stay back to talk to Ann Templeton."

Cindy turned to Watch. "Then we are back in time."

Watch nodded. "By just coming here, over the mountains, we passed through the time warp without knowing it."

"I need to know what's happening here," Bryce said impatiently.

Watch and Cindy explained about the two groups of aliens, the battle, and the big metal box that was sitting in the volcanic chamber at the end of the cave. Bryce listened closely and when they were done he thought for a minute with his eyes closed. When he opened them, he questioned Watch and Cindy more.

"Does it look as if this new group of aliens is trying to stop the metal box from working?" he asked.

"How should we know?" Cindy said. "They just look ugly—that's all we know."

"I suspect these new aliens are here to destroy the box," Watch said carefully. "Or at least to stop it from doing whatever the first group of aliens planned."

"Why do you say that?" Bryce asked.

"The nice-looking aliens appeared to be setting up the device," Watch explained. "These new guys seem to be figuring out how to turn it off."

"But what is this device?" Sally wanted to know.

"It would take tremendous power to warp time," Bryce said. "But even if you were to put together all the nuclear bombs we have, their power wouldn't equal the power of one huge volcanic eruption. For that reason, I think the eruption of this volcano is a key to explain the formation of the time warp that exists between now and our usual time." He paused. "I think this metal box you have described is definitely a bomb and that it was placed here by the first group of aliens to ignite the volcano and cause the time warp."

"Then you think these ugly aliens are here to stop the explosion and prevent the time warp?" Sally asked.

Bryce hesitated. "That's my opinion. It makes sense."

Sally was relieved. "Then we can just leave and return to our time. The problem is being taken care of by these ugly aliens."

Bryce paused. "I think so."

Watch shook his head. "The reverse could be true. This device might have been brought here by the first aliens to stop the volcano from exploding."

"That's a possibility," Bryce admitted. "But it's unlikely. There's a better chance the device is being used as a trigger for an explosion rather than as a method of stopping the explosion."

"Why should this volcanic explosion cause a time warp?" Watch asked.

"Because this volcano is situated exactly where Madeline Templeton's grave is, in our time," Bryce explained. "This spot is already unstable as far as space and time are concerned."

Watch was impressed. "It is possible the old witch had herself buried in that exact spot because it was unstable."

"Why would she do that?" Cindy asked.

"Maybe so she could come back to life after she was dead," Watch said.

"We can't worry about that now," Sally said. "If Bryce says these ugly aliens are taking care of the problem then I believe him. Let's get out of here."

"But we can't leave until we're sure," Watch said.

There was a movement in the shadows.

A dark figure with a fat head and black slits for eyes appeared.

It pointed a mean-looking weapon at them.

"Oh," Sally whispered. "I guess we won't be leaving."

8

ADAM SAT IN MS. ANN TEMPLETON'S CASTLE
in what he assumed was a living room of sorts. There
was a long table with chairs. A row of burning torches
led away from the room down a narrow stone hallway.
There was no other furniture in the room and no sign
of her trolls. As before, when he had entered her castle,
Adam wasn't sure how he had gotten from one room to
the other. Doorways just seemed to open and close at her
bidding.

She had been waiting for him at the front door.

As if she had been expecting him.

And even though her castle had just been attacked
by a murderous dinosaur, and she had lost several of her

trolls, she didn't appear to be upset. Indeed, it was almost as if she had enjoyed the encounter with the tyrannosaurus. She sat at one end of the table directly opposite him and wore a slightly amused smile. She looked as beautiful as ever, with her long black hair and her bewitching green eyes. She wore a long red robe, a thin gold necklace that held a glittering emerald at the base of her throat.

"You're wondering why I am not upset," she said.

"Yes. Can you read my mind?" he asked.

"Yes. But don't be embarrassed. You have a good mind, Adam. It will take you far."

He shook his head. "I don't know how far I'll go. Today, I'm just worried that we don't all end up dead." He paused. "Can you help us drive off the dinosaurs?"

"No."

He had been afraid she would say that.

"But you're so powerful," he said. "You scared the tyrannosaurus away."

"I scared it away, I didn't kill it. Also, there are many dinosaurs now walking the streets of Spooksville. How do you expect me to deal with them all?"

Adam felt miserable. "But you can't just let the city be destroyed. This is your home as well as mine."

Ann Templeton chuckled softly. "Don't sound so glum. I don't necessarily have to intervene for the town to be saved. What about your friends? They are all busy working on the time warp."

"Then it is a time warp that brought the dinosaurs?"

"Yes."

Adam paused. "Do you know if Cindy is all right?"

Ann Templeton was sympathetic. "You're worried that the pterodactyl killed her?"

Adam nodded. "We did everything we could to save her, but the creature was just too big and mean."

"I know you did." She paused and put her right hand up to her forehead. For a moment she closed her eyes and did some kind of rapid breathing. Then she opened her eyes again and stared at him. She spoke in a soft but serious tone. "Cindy is alive but she is in danger. All your friends are."

Adam jumped up. "Then I should go and rescue them!"

She gestured for him to sit back down. "Not yet. You came here for a reason. What is it?"

He slowly sat back down. "I wanted your help in stopping the dinosaurs."

"You wanted advice as well. I can give you that. But can't you see that I can't always be running to rescue you and your friends? You have to meet the dangers of Spooksville head on, as you have been doing. It is the only way you can be prepared."

Adam hesitated. "Prepared for what?"

Ann Templeton smiled. "You are being prepared for a great destiny. All your friends are. But I won't tell you what it is. If I do, that would ruin the surprise."

Adam was stunned. He wasn't even sure what the word *destiny* meant.

"But can you tell me why Spooksville is always so spooky?" he asked.

She thought silently for a minute. "Watch asked me that question not long ago. He came here for advice on how to deal with the Wicked Cat. Did he tell you?"

"Yes, ma'am."

"I did not give him a specific answer. Once again, you can only be prepared for your destiny in ignorance."

"I don't understand," Adam said.

"It doesn't matter, you will." She paused again, and it seemed as if her mind was far away. Then she stirred and looked over at him. "Bum has told you about the ancient wars that occurred on this planet, between Atlantis and Lemuria?"

"Yes. He told us a little about it when the Cold People attacked."

Ann Templeton chuckled. "*Them.* I think they're going to be back one day."

"I sure hope not. They were hard to get rid of." Adam

73

paused. "But I would like to know more about Atlantis and Lemuria."

She nodded. "Bum told you that Spooksville is the last remaining bit of Lemuria, and that is true. But the ancient war between the two great continents was only a reflection of a greater war that was happening in the stars. In fact, that war continues to this day, and some of whom you call aliens want the earth to survive and others do not. Do you understand?"

"Are you saying the time warp was opened by the bad aliens who want to wipe out the earth?"

"In a manner of speaking. Certainly by allowing dinosaurs to invade our time they would be able to wipe us out without having to expend a lot of energy. But I'm not saying the aliens deliberately did something to open the time warp."

"I don't understand."

She smiled. "Do you want me to spell it out for you? Do you think that would be best?"

Adam hesitated. "No. I guess I have to figure it out for myself. The bad aliens probably wanted the rip in time but didn't really do anything to make it happen?"

Ann Templeton stood. "That's the riddle. But don't worry, you will figure it out, with the help of your friends. You always do."

Adam also stood. "But how can I get to them in time to help save them?"

She threw her head back and laughed. "So many questions? Very well, Adam, at least you ask me politely. I will give you a little more information. A few more secrets." Bidding him to come close, she leaned over and touched his wounded shoulder. "But first you must be made whole if you are going to be a hero."

Her fingers covered his wound for a few seconds.

Adam felt a delicious warmth spread through his whole body.

Then she removed her hand and his injury was healed!

He gasped "How did you do that?"

"That is one secret I can't tell you today." Then she lowered her head more and whispered in his ear. "But there are others secrets you may know, Adam. I will tell you how to open the Secret Path without having to walk all over town. How to use it so that you can travel in time. Even back as far as seventy million years."

9

ADAM MATERIALIZED INTO A HOT DARK cave. Off to his right he saw a faint red glow and walked carefully toward it. He didn't have far to go before he came to a wide underground chamber lit with bubbling pools of lava. In the center of the chamber was a group of four fat-headed aliens standing around a desk-size metal box. They seemed to have finished working and appeared to be in the midst of congratulating one another on a job well done.

Behind them, chained to the far wall, Adam saw his friends and Bryce Poole.

Adam wasn't ready yet to accept Bryce as a true friend. Even though Ann Templeton had told him that

Cindy was alive, Adam was nevertheless relieved to see her with his own eyes. But he was not happy that the fat-headed aliens had captured his friends. He figured these must be the bad aliens, and knew he had to move with caution. If he had any doubts about the latter, he had only to look at the floor in front of him where the bodies of the other aliens lay sprawled in a pile.

Curiously enough the dead aliens still had their laser pistols in their holsters. Of course the bad aliens probably figured they didn't need to disarm corpses. Also, the bad aliens probably believed they had rounded up all the intruding humans. Adam smiled to himself at their oversight. None of the fat heads were looking his way, so he had only to reach out. In moments he had a laser pistol in his hand.

"How do I put this thing on Stun?" Adam whispered to himself. There were clearly three settings, but he couldn't tell the Kill setting from the Blow Up Everything setting. It was not as though he wanted to kill the ugly aliens. He simply wanted to free his friends and save Spooksville. But not only did he not know how to use the laser pistol, he didn't know how to save his friends without the aliens seeing him.

Then Adam realized that the three caves that entered the chamber must be interconnected. He decided to walk back the way he had come to see if he could swing around the aliens and come at them from the far side. Even though his friends were chained to the far wall, they were close to the largest of the cave openings.

Adam's insight proved accurate. Ten minutes later he was creeping up on the chamber from the other side. The aliens were still gathered around the big metal box, chatting in scratchy voices that sounded like CD's being played with sandpaper. His friends were only a few feet away. But there was no way Adam was emerging from the safe shadows of the cave to talk to them. He listened for a moment before speaking, and was pleased to hear Sally complaining to Bryce.

"How could you think these fat heads were here to save us from the dinosaurs?" she said.

"It seemed a logical assumption at the time," Bryce said.

"Yeah. It was logical right up until they chained us to these rocks," Sally said.

"Hindsight is always twenty-twenty," Bryce said.

"And common sense is usually right most of the time," Sally snapped. "I tell you, if an alien is ugly he is probably evil."

"If only Adam was here," Cindy said with a sigh, "he would save us."

"Adam was afraid to come here," Bryce said.

"I don't believe that," Watch said. "Adam's not afraid of anything."

"I wouldn't go that far," Adam whispered.

They jumped at his words, but were wise enough to keep their voices down. Watch leaned over from where he was chained to the wall and peered into the dark cave.

"Is that you, Adam?" he whispered.

"Yes. I'm here. But try not to look my way."

Watch straightened up quickly. "You're right."

"We're saved," Sally gushed quietly.

"I knew Adam would come," Cindy said.

"He hasn't saved us yet," Bryce muttered.

"I have a hand laser," Adam whispered. "I took it from those dead aliens over there. But I'm not sure how to use the thing."

"I think you just have to aim and fire," Watch said.

"I don't want to have to kill the fat heads," Adam explained. "I don't know how to set the laser for Stun."

"Just kill them," Sally hissed. "They're trying to kill us."

"Whatever setting the gun was on when you took it," Watch said, "that setting probably kills. When the others were attacked, they were not just trying to stun the fat heads."

"But there are two more settings," Adam whispered.

"You'll just have to guess which one is Stun," Watch said.

"But whatever you do," Bryce added, "when you fire at them be careful not to hit the metal box. We're all convinced it's a bomb of some type."

"Adam knows that," Sally said. "He's not stupid."

Bryce was annoyed at her. "You know, Sally, you're a fair-weather friend. I make one little mistake and you jump all over me."

"Join the club," Watch muttered.

"I'm going to open fire now," Adam said, changing the setting on the laser and taking aim. "Wish me luck."

"Good luck, Adam," Bryce said.

"So Bryce likes Adam now that Adam is saving his life," Sally muttered.

"Quiet," Watch snapped. "Let him concentrate."

Adam found it difficult to focus. The aliens were all so close to the metal box. He didn't see how he could shoot them without hitting it. Also, he continued to worry that he was about to kill the aliens, whether they were evil or not, and without fair warning. Yet in the end, he had to push all that aside. He had come here to do a job and he had to succeed. Too many people were depending on him. Bracing his shooting arm on a rock protruding from the cave wall, he managed to steady his aim.

Adam squeezed the trigger.

A bolt of red light hit the tallest alien and it crumbled to the floor.

Adam didn't know if the creature was dead or merely unconscious.

But he kept on shooting.

Two more blasts and two more aliens went down.

But the last of the fat heads had managed to draw its weapon and get off a shot. Adam saw a burst of red light and then the wall beside him exploded in a shower of burning sparks. He was knocked to the side, onto the floor, and the laser pistol flew from his grasp.

"Adam!" his friends screamed.

Adam was stunned but still awake. He scrambled for his laser in the dark of the cave as six laser blasts soared over his head. It was good that he had been knocked down or else he would be dead already. But he still had the advantage because he didn't think the alien could see him. Adam would need only one good shot to finish off the bad guys.

Adam's hand bumped against the laser.

He raised it while still lying on the floor of the cave, propping his right arm up with his left palm, sighting along the barrel. For a moment the alien paused, perhaps thinking Adam was finished. It was in that moment that Adam shot it, a clean hit to the chest.

The alien went down.

"Adam!" his friends cheered.

Adam jumped up and ran into the chamber. The chains the aliens had used to secure his friends were long. Adam told them all to stand back while he fired at the point where the metal met the stone. In less than a minute they were all free; the handcuffs broke open as the chains shattered. Naturally, Adam freed Bryce last, but the guy didn't seem to mind.

When they were finished hugging and congratulating one another on being alive, they still had the problem of the metal box. What were they supposed to do with it?

"I still think it is a bomb set to trigger the volcano and cause the time warp," Bryce said.

Watch studied the control panel. It appeared dead.

"But you are then implying that these evil aliens came here to stop it from exploding," Watch said. "Because it sure looks like they turned it off."

Bryce hesitated. "That must be the case."

Sally shook her head. "I don't think these fat heads came here for anybody's benefit but their own."

"What should we do?" Cindy asked anxiously. "Sally says people are dying right now in Spooksville."

"No," Watch corrected. "They are dying seventy million years in the future in Spooksville."

"It's the same difference to them," Sally quipped.

"I say we just leave," Bryce said. "I think everything will be all right."

"No," Adam said softly, but with confidence.

He remembered what Ann Templeton had told him.

The riddle. The bad aliens would not deliberately do something to open the time warp. Yet they would open it nevertheless. The solution was obvious.

"This is a bomb," Adam continued. "But it is a bomb that halts the full eruption of the volcano. It was never designed to trigger it. The first group of aliens came here to *prevent* the time warp. And yet, it was *destined* to happen. The bad aliens did not really cause the dinosaurs to invade Spooksville."

"What does *destined* mean?" Cindy asked.

"It was meant to happen," Sally explained. "Can that be true?"

"Yes," Adam said. "But in another sense the bad aliens did cause the time warp because they stopped the good aliens from completing their task. Now what I think we have to do is restart this bomb."

"But how would a bomb halt the eruption?" Bryce asked.

"It could cause this volcanic cone to cave in on itself," Watch said. "Or else it could blow a hole in the side of the cone and allow it to vent its pressure over time, instead of in one huge explosion."

Bryce nodded. "That's logical. But it doesn't mean it's necessarily true."

"I feel it's true," Adam said. "And I am willing to trust that feeling."

"And I'm willing to trust Adam," Sally said defiantly.

Bryce was not positive. "All right, let's assume Adam is correct. How do we turn this bomb back on?"

Watch shook his head as he studied the control panel. "It could take us a year to figure out these buttons. I'm afraid to push any of them. The wrong one might set the bomb off in our faces."

"Then it's hopeless," Cindy said. "We should get out of here while we can."

"It's never hopeless," Adam said, and his eyes strayed to the corner where the good aliens had been piled up. Maybe they were all only stunned, he wasn't sure. Adam only knew that one of them had begun to stir.

10

THEY RAN TO THE HANDSOME ALIEN AS HE
blinked and tried to get up. Adam and Watch helped
him into a sitting position and for a few moments it
seemed he didn't know where he was. He put a hand to
his head and grimaced in pain. But the spasm seemed to
pass and then he smiled and nodded.

"Do you speak English?" Adam asked.

The man shook his head.

"But you understand a little?" Watch said.

The man held up a finger and thumb, holding them
slightly apart.

He understood very little.

Adam pointed to the metal box. "Can you make that work?"

The man nodded and tried to get up. But he needed their help to stay on his feet. The bad aliens' guns—even set to stun—must have been pretty powerful. Adam hoped the bad aliens that lay sprawled across the floor were not dead. He also hoped they didn't wake up any time soon.

They helped the alien over to the metal box. There Cindy pointed to her chest and said, "Cindy." Then she gestured to the alien, and he in turn pointed to himself.

"Traelle," he said.

"Traelle," Cindy repeated. She then completed the introductions. "This is Adam, Watch, Sally, and Bryce. We are pleased to meet you, Traelle."

"And we hope you are not preparing to destroy our world," Sally added.

"Sally!" Cindy snapped. "That's rude."

"How can you talk about being rude to an alien?" Sally asked. "Oh his planet spitting in someone's face might be the height of etiquette."

"Please don't spit in his face," Bryce muttered.

"I was just going to say that," Watch said.

"Traelle," Adam said, tapping the metal box on the top. "Will this get rid of the dinosaurs from our time?"

Traelle just stared at him.

"Dinosaurs," Sally said, and made a loud growling sound.

Traelle first nodded, made the same growling sound—although not as well as Sally, who seemed a natural when it came to growls—and then shook his head. Adam spoke to the others.

"I think he is saying that he understands what dinosaurs are," Adam said. "And that with the metal box there will be no more dinosaurs in our time."

"Or maybe no more on the earth," Bryce said darkly. "It is remotely possible this bomb is designed to blow up the whole planet."

"That's one way of solving our problem," Watch observed.

"Why do you always have to look on the gloomy side of things?" Sally asked Bryce.

"That's the kettle calling the pot black," Cindy remarked.

Adam looked up at Traelle and the alien smiled at him with such warmth that Adam found it impossible to believe their visitor could ever intentionally harm anyone. Traelle patted his arm.

"Adam," he said.

Adam patted his arm back. "Friend," he said.

Traelle nodded. "Friend."

"Looks like they're getting along nicely," Watch said. "Traelle may as well turn the device back on. If it blows us up or saves us—at least we'll have a resolution to the day's crisis."

"Wait," Bryce said. "If he does arm the device, show him with your watch that we want at least two hours to get clear of this place."

"Good idea," Adam said. "But maybe Watch should show him."

"I am a time specialist," Watch agreed. With a series of gestures, Watch tried to explain to Traelle that they didn't want the bomb to go off in their faces. Traelle quickly nodded. It seemed he had already thought of the problem.

Traelle set to work on the control board. Soon it was up and humming. A faint vibration began to fill the underground chamber. Traelle pointed to a series of fluctuating symbols, which flashed against a gray screen in a rainbow of colors. The symbols looked as if they could be numbers. Then Traelle gestured to one of Watch's four watches. His meaning was clear.

The countdown was on.

"Thanks," Adam said, offering Traelle his hand. The alien clasped Adam's hand with both of his hands and once more Adam felt a wave of warmth sweep over him. He realized what it reminded him of—Ms. Ann Templeton's touch, when she had healed him.

As Traelle let go he gestured to the other aliens—the good ones and the bad ones—lying on the floor. To their immense surprise he turned his thumb up. Once again his meaning was clear. He would take care of the fallen, even when it came to the enemy.

It was time for them to return to their own time and space. They walked out of the chamber through the largest cave and soon reached the flying saucer. Actually, there were two flying saucers now. The bad guys had, of course, landed while they were inside.

Naturally they started to argue about how they should go home. Sally and Bryce wanted to go through the Secret Path. They said that was the quickest and safest way back. But Watch was adamant that he had to return the truck to the place he had found it.

"But I don't care if the rest of you take the Secret Path," Watch said. "I can return the truck myself."

"And along the way you might get attacked by who knows how many dinosaurs," Cindy said. "You can't go alone. I'm going with you."

"Like you're a fine one to have along during a dinosaur attack," Sally muttered.

CHRISTOPHER PIKE

"If Watch feels he has to return the truck," Adam said, "then I'm going with him."

"This is ridiculous," Sally complained. "Cindy has already said what is wrong with this idea. We spent half the morning fighting off just one pterodactyl. For all we know a whole flock of them could swoop down on us before we get back over the mountains. I say we take the Secret Path and call it a day."

"But not to return the truck is stealing," Watch said.

"You just saved the world!" Sally exclaimed. "The owner of the truck should want to give you the truck as a gift."

Watch remained stubborn. "I took it and I have to return it. But why don't you and Bryce just take the Secret Path home? None of us will hold it against you."

"Yeah," Cindy said playfully. "You cowards."

"I've never been called a coward before," Bryce muttered.

Sally glanced at him. "What do you want to do? I know these guys. They'll harass me for the rest of my life if I show any sign of weakness."

Bryce shrugged. "Then if we're going to get killed, let's get killed together."

Watch patted him on the back. "Maybe you can be one of us, Bryce. Sally is already insulting you and you're developing a fatalistic attitude."

11

THEY HAD BEEN SEARCHING FOR MORE THAN an hour, and it looked as if they had made the wrong choice. They couldn't find the truck, or rather, Watch couldn't find it since he was the only one who knew where he had parked it. But he wasn't entirely to blame. The truck was blue, as were millions of primordial leaves. The truck was just another big flower in an endless sea of dinosaur forest.

"Maybe we should go back," Sally said. "Take the Secret Path. We don't know how long we have."

"I know," Watch said, wiping the sweat from his brow. The forest was hot and humid, and they were all drenched in perspiration and painfully thirsty. "I understood Traelle's sign language. We have twenty minutes left."

The group howled in amazement.

"Why didn't you tell us?" Adam asked.

"I didn't want to worry you," Watch said.

"Worry us?" Sally screamed. "You're going to kill us! We have to go back to the volcano now."

Adam glanced at the distant volcanic cone. "I don't think we can get there in twenty minutes."

Sally began to pace. "Oh, that's great. That's just swell. Here we had a secret doorway only seconds away that led to freedom and pleasure and we chose to take a path home that leads through danger just to save a stupid blue truck."

"I kind of like that truck," Watch said.

"Fine!" Sally shouted. "I hope Saint Peter gives you one to play with in heaven!"

"Stop yelling," Adam said. "We have to figure a way out of this."

"I like to yell when I'm scared!" Sally yelled. "It calms me down!"

"The only way out of this predicament is to find the truck in the next few minutes," Bryce said quietly. "Watch, which direction did you hike right after you parked?"

Watch pointed. "Toward that peak. Isn't that the one you were on, Cindy?"

Cindy shook her head. "No. It was that one over there. Don't you remember?"

Sally continued to fret. "We have the blind leading the blind."

Watch paused and wiped off his glasses. A moment later he settled them back on his nose and nodded in surprise.

"You're right, Cindy," Watch said. "My sense of direction got turned around. My lenses keep steaming up in this place."

"So does this mean you know where the truck is now?" Adam asked, praying that his friend said yes. Thankfully Watch nodded and pointed to their left.

"It should be just over there," he said.

They found the truck five minutes later.

Fifteen minutes to detonation.

There were five of them now, rather than the usual four. They couldn't all sit in the front. Actually, the truck had bucket seats. Only two could be comfortable up front. Cindy joined Watch in the driver's compartment while Sally, Adam, and Bryce bounced in the back. The road home was rough because, well, actually there was no road. They were all amazed that Watch had managed to push the truck as far back into the primeval forest as he had.

Time flew by. It always did when one was in a hurry.

Seven minutes to detonation. Still no sign of Spooksville.

"Are you sure you're heading the right way?" Adam called to Watch.

"Not absolutely positive," Watch replied.

"We're running out of time," Sally said for the tenth time.

"We're running out of gas as well," Watch said.

Sally screamed at the sky. "I hate this!"

But maybe Sally shouldn't have screamed so loud. She might have called attention to themselves. From out of the low hanging clouds a screeching pterodactyl suddenly appeared. And it was probably *their* pterodactyl because Watch noticed it had a bruise on its head from the boulder he had dropped on it. He said as much to the others.

"You knocked it out?" Sally asked in amazement. "You had it helpless? Why didn't you just kill it?"

"It's a mother pterodactyl," Watch called out the truck window. "It has babies to feed."

"It has babies it wants to feed us to!" Sally shouted. "Adam! Do you still have that laser pistol?"

Adam pulled out the weapon. "I do."

Sally tried to grab it from him. When she failed she fidgeted anxiously as she stared up at the sky. The pterodactyl had gone into another one of its famous dives and there was no mistaking its target.

"Shoot it then!" Sally yelled. "And don't give me any idiotic lines about not wanting to harm it. Believe me— it wants to harm us."

Adam hesitated. "How many babies does it have?" he asked Cindy.

"There were four eggs in its nest," Cindy replied, her head stuck out the window. She was also staring up at the pterodactyl with fear in her eyes. "One of them hatched just as I was leaving. It scratched my leg."

Five minutes to detonation.

Watch spoke up. "I think I see signs of Spooksville!"

It was true, the scenery up ahead was beginning to look less weird.

But the pterodactyl didn't care. It was coming fast.

"If you keep the laser on Stun," Bryce suggested to Adam, "a few shots might discourage it from attacking."

"No!" Sally cried. "Put the laser on full power! Blow the monster out the sky! It tried to kill us this morning! We don't owe it any tenderness!"

Adam came to a decision. Raising the laser, he took aim along the barrel.

"I'll try to stun it," he muttered.

"That won't even slow it down," Sally muttered.

Adam fired. He was turning into a good shot.

A direct hit to the pterodactyl's face.

Unfortunately Sally was right.

The creature screeched louder, and kept coming.

"You tried to be a Good Samaritan," Sally pleaded with Adam. "But this flying lizard is not a moral creature. It's not going to reward you for your altruistic laser pistol settings. Use full power, Adam, please?"

Three minutes to detonation.

Ten seconds to pterodactyl dinner.

Adam swallowed thickly. He shouted to Watch.

"Will full power kill it?" he asked.

"It will probably roast its guts," Watch shouted back.

"How about the middle setting?" Bryce asked, beginning to squirm where he sat. The pterodactyl filled the sky now, its screeching ringing in their ears. "You can hurt it without killing it, Adam."

"Yeah!" Sally agreed. From the look on her face she appeared on the verge of jumping from the truck. "Hurt it! Don't kill it if you can't. Just make it go away!"

"Okay," Adam said reluctantly.

He readjusted the pistol setting and took aim.

He fired. A thick bolt of red energy flashed toward the giant lizard.

Another bulls-eye. The pterodactyl screamed and veered to one side.

Two minutes to detonation.

But the pterodactyl was only hurt. It wasn't finished with them.

Once more it started after them. But this time it was coming in low.

Bryce said it for all of them.

"You might have to kill it if we're to survive," he said.

"Haven't I been saying that all along?" Sally gasped.

There were normal trees just up ahead.

One minute to detonation.

Adam adjusted the laser to full power.

The pterodactyl was only a hundred yards behind them, already flexing its claws. But Watch had managed to pick up speed. As they neared the edge of the time warp, the ground had begun to smooth out. The pterodactyl was coming fast but it was having to strain to catch them. Its huge wings pounded the air as it flapped furiously. Yet it seemed it would catch them. It cut the distance between them in half, to fifty yards, then to twenty. They could smell it now, even see into its huge red and black eyes, and see the hunger in its slobbering mouth.

Thirty seconds to detonation.

Thirteen seconds to pterodactyl attack.

Three hundred yards to normal scenery.

Adam raised the laser for a third time and took aim.

Watch floored the truck accelerator.

"Shoot it!" Sally cried.

Adam fired. The red energy spewed forth.

But at that exact moment they hit a bump and he missed.

Fifteen seconds to detonation.

The monster opened its beak wide.

Two seconds to pterodactyl dessert.

One hundred yards to Spooksville's city limit.

For the fourth time Adam began to squeeze the laser trigger.

But suddenly the pterodactyl began to gag.

Adam had to blink several times to understand the reason.

Sally had removed her shoe and thrown it into the monster's mouth.

The pterodactyl veered away.

Coughing like a parrot with a peanut stuck in its throat.

Sally shrugged as Adam and Bryce stared at her in amazement.

"It worked for Watch this morning," she said casually. "Besides, somebody had to save us. I'm not kidding, I'm never going into battle again with a bunch of pacifists like you guys."

They crossed over into normal Spooksville.

There was a blinding flash of light behind them.

And the primeval forest vanished.

Epilogue

THEY PARKED THE TRUCK WHERE THEY HAD found it and left a note on the dashboard saying that they would be happy to pay for the window they had broken, and for the gasoline they had consumed. Indeed, they had had to roll to the desired spot on the deserted road. They had run out of gas not long after cresting the mountains directly behind Spooksville.

As they walked into town they immediately understood that the dinosaur attack had not happened for their neighbors, not in this new reality. Nothing was out of place, nobody was crying. Adam had been right. Because they had helped fix the problem in the past, it had ceased to exist in the present. No one had died, they realized, and that was the most important thing.

But as they hiked past the witch's castle they found Ms. Ann Templeton out front. She was watering the alligators and crocodiles in her moat. She waved to them as they walked by and called them over. They noticed she had a bunch of tiny toys in her hands. She laughed when she saw their puzzled expressions and held the toys up for them to see.

They were tiny dinosaurs.

Each a perfect model of a creature they had met that day.

Ann Templeton smiled. "I thought you might like these as souvenirs."

But they turned her down. Even Adam.

Some creatures in Spooksville were better left forgotten.

TURN THE PAGE FOR A SNEAK PEEK AT
SPOOKSVILLE #12: THE HIDDEN BEAST

It was Leah Poole, Bryce Poole's cousin, who brought the gang the treasure map. The fact that Leah was related to Bryce made Adam Freeman and Watch suspicious. Even though Adam and Watch had shared a couple of adventures with Bryce—one on the other side of the Secret Path, the other when prehistoric dinosaurs invaded Spooksville—the guys simply did not trust Bryce. The fact that he said he wanted to share a treasure with them made them trust him less.

Even the girls had their doubts. While fighting the invasion of dinosaurs, Bryce had made a few bad calls that Sally Wilcox had not forgiven. But to Sally's credit—perhaps a credit to her greed—she was the one most interested in the treasure hunt. Cindy Makey, on the other hand, didn't understand why Leah Poole would go to complete strangers and offer them half of a supposedly fabulous treasure in return for a little help. Cindy liked Bryce, but his cousin was another matter. Yet maybe Cindy's distrust of Leah was partly because Leah was so pretty, with her sandy brown hair and pearl white teeth. Prettier, in fact, than Cindy.

At least that was what Sally later said.

They were in their favorite doughnut shop when Bryce walked in and hit them with the idea of the treasure hunt. Leah was outside for the moment, out of sight. Apparently Bryce wanted to soften them up on the idea first. But he hadn't been talking long when they were all over him with questions.

"Where did this map come from?" Adam asked.

"Where did the treasure come from?" Watch asked.

"Where did Leah come from?" Sally asked.

"Yeah," Cindy echoed.

Bryce shook his head. "One question at a time. First, my cousin was born in Spooksville but moved away five years ago. She's seventeen now, so she left here with my uncle when she was our age. It was her father, Uncle Charlie, who gave her the map just before he died. That was only two months ago—she's still getting over the loss of her dad. It was her dad's dying wish that she return here and find the treasure. Uncle Charlie was flat broke when he died, and Leah has no way to support herself."

"She has no mother?" Cindy asked sympathetically. Blond and cute, Cindy was the gentlest one in the group, except when it came to dealing with Sally.

"Her mother died when she was two," Bryce said. "Anyway, she returned here with this map but . . ."

"Yes?" Adam asked when Bryce didn't finish. Although the shortest and the newest to town, Adam usually led the group.

"It's in code," Bryce said reluctantly.

"And you can't figure it out?" Sally asked. Sally had long brown hair and liked to ask hard questions.

Bryce hesitated. "I am having some difficulties."

"Wonders never cease," Watch said, glancing at one of the four watches he always wore on his arms.

"Where did Leah's father get the map?" Adam asked.

"I don't know," Bryce said. "But he grew up in Spooksville and lived most of his life here. He was adventurous when he was little. I'm not surprised that he found a treasure map."

"But if he's had the map for a while," Watch said, "why didn't he go for the treasure himself?"

"I'm not sure how long he had the map," Bryce said. "I'm only guessing when he got it. He died before Leah could really ask him about it."

Watch frowned. "Are you saying he gave it to her with his dying breath?"

"I wouldn't go that far," Bryce said. "I only know that Leah doesn't know where the map came from."

"Then how does she know it's genuine?" Sally asked.

"Her father swore it was," Bryce said. "I knew the guy. He was honest."

"But we still don't get the deal," Adam said. "Why should Leah share half the treasure with us in exchange for our help? You'll be able to decipher the code without us."

Bryce sighed. "I've been studying the code for the last two weeks and haven't been able crack it yet."

"So it's both a map and directions?" Watch asked.

"Yes," Bryce said. "Leah's outside with the map. She's willing to show it to you, if you swear to keep it secret."

The gang, the inner four, all looked at one another. Sally was the first to speak. "I suppose it couldn't hurt," she said.

"Maybe," Adam answered carefully. "But I've got a funny feeling about this treasure map, even before I see it. Does it hint that there's any danger in chasing after this treasure?"

Again Bryce hesitated. "Sort of. The instructions are weird. There is a hint of danger."

"But why does Leah want us to help?" Watch asked. "We're only kids."

"I told her about you guys," Bryce said. "When it comes to handling bizarre adventures, I said you're the best." He added, "I'm trying to help you, even though you've accused me in the past of acting like I could do everything myself."

"Who accused you?" Adam asked. "Not me."

"Your tone accused me," Bryce said. "Besides, you told me you didn't trust me."

"I think you were the one who said that," Adam said.

"It doesn't matter," Sally said, showing a rare ability to compromise. "We can see the map and then decide if we want to get involved. Who knows—even we may not be able to decode it."

"But if we do decode it," Watch said firmly, "the deal can't change. We get half the treasure."

Bryce nodded. "That's fine with me. If Leah's father was right, there should be so much treasure it won't matter how many share it." Bryce stood. "I'll go get my cousin."

While he was gone, the gang talked.

"Now that I think about it," Watch said, "I do

remember this Leah. She was tall, even as a little kid, and had a sharp mind. I'm surprised she hasn't been able to decode the message."

"Was she a nice person?" Cindy asked.

Watch shrugged. "I didn't really know her."

"Am I a nice person?" Sally asked Cindy with a trace of sarcasm.

Cindy looked her straight in the eye. "One or two days out of the month."

"We only have a few days before school starts," Watch said. "We might want to go on one last summer adventure—all together," he added meaningfully.

Leah appeared a moment later. As Watch remembered, she was tall, with thick red lips and curly hair that seemed to change color as she turned her head in the bright sunlight pouring in through the window. But even though she was five years older, and very pretty, she seemed apprehensive to meet them. She stood stiffly while Bryce introduced her. It was Adam who had to suggest she take a seat. In her hands she carried a brown piece of parchment. As she settled down in the booth across from them, she clutched the paper close to her chest. Watch tried to put her at ease.

"We're not going to steal it from you," he joked. "At least not right away."

Leah smiled thinly. "I haven't told anyone about this map except Bryce. I'm sure you can understand why."

Adam waved his hand. "We're good at keeping secrets. We've had aliens and witches confide in us."

"Not that we confided in them," Sally muttered.

Bryce spoke to Leah. "I'd trust these guys with my life. In fact, they've saved my life. You can trust them with your inheritance."

"Do you think of your treasure map as an inheritance?" Watch asked Leah. "That might not be such a good idea."

"What Watch means is that we might not find anything," Adam said quickly. "We don't want you to be disappointed."

Leah hesitated. "My father said if I could decipher the map, I would find wealth beyond imagination."

"How come he failed to decipher the code?" Sally asked.

"It's not easy," Leah said. "But Bryce tells me you guys are all brilliant."

"Three-quarters of us are," Sally said, glancing at Cindy.

"Let's see the map and we'll show you how brilliant we are," Watch said, obviously anxious to try his wits on the code. Once more Leah hesitated, but then slowly she laid the map down on the table. But it was Adam who spread it open.

The map was simple. On the left side was a series of triangles that seemed to represent mountains. Opposite the triangles was a set of wavy lines that appeared to be the ocean. In between was a bunch of stick trees and what looked like poorly drawn rocks. There was a large X in the middle of the triangles. That was it.

But the clues were bizarre, far from clear.

They were actually written as a poem.

> When the morning and evening lady stands at
> her tallest.
> The shadow of the white light of love shall
> falleth.
>
> In a line of darkness on the door of the smallest.
> In a hidden spot on the tallest.
>
> Therein lie the jewels that speak in dreams.
> The crystals that whisper words that are more
> than they seem.
>
> But beware the ancient pet.
> The fire that burns yet.

She who remembers old debts.
She whose breath melts every net.

"Nice rhymes," Adam said as he finished reading it out loud. "But I haven't a clue what any of it means."

"Of course you don't," Watch said quickly, taking hold of the map. "We have to study it for a while. But one thing is clear to me. If this is a map of Spooksville, it's reversed. See how the mountains are on the left side, the west side, when they should be on the east side?" Watch frowned. "They're not only reversed. I think they're inverted as well."

"What do you mean?" Cindy asked. "Don't *reversed* and *inverted* mean the same thing?"

"Not exactly," Watch said. "I believe the map was drawn with the help of a mirror. That if we look at its reflection in a mirror we'll see where the X is really supposed to be. Sally, do you know where we can get a mirror?"

"It's not necessary," Bryce said, reaching into his pocket and pulling out a piece of notebook paper. "I've already redrawn the map while looking in a mirror." He opened the folded paper and laid it on the table beside the old parchment. It was an exact copy of the original, but reversed. Bryce smiled. "Very good, Watch. It took me hours studying the map to realize it had been inverted."

Sally wasn't smiling. "Why didn't you volunteer that information from the start?"

Bryce shrugged. "I wanted to see if one of you guys noticed it."

"That's not the way a team works," Adam said in a flat tone. "If you know other things about the map, please tell us now so we don't waste valuable time."

Bryce shook his head. "That's all I know."

Watch continued to study the parchment and the notebook paper intently. He spoke to Bryce with his next question. "But do you know where the X is located?"

Bryce hesitated. "Only approximately."

"Where?" Sally asked.

Watch pointed to the row of triangles. "This is back in the mountains, in a minor range of peaks called the Teeth."

Cindy shuddered. "Why are they called that?"

"Because they're really pointy peaks," Bryce said. "And close together."

"We assume that's the reason," Watch said darkly, staring at Bryce. "This map refers to an ancient pet. Do you have any idea what that means?"

"No," Bryce said. "I haven't been able to figure out the clues."

"Yeah," Sally said sarcastically. "And when you walked in here, you said you didn't know the treasure was located back in the Teeth either."

Bryce held her eye. "I brought Leah and this map to you guys because I trust you. Now gimme a break, will ya?"

"We'll think about it," Sally said.

Adam held up his hand. "Let's look at the clues one by one. What about the first line? 'When the morning and the evening lady stands at her tallest.' That's clearly referring to a special time. Maybe a special time of the day, maybe a special time of the year." He paused. "But which lady is connected to the morning and the evening?"

Cindy shook her head. "I haven't the slightest idea."

"I studied all the different goddesses in mythology," Bryce said. "I couldn't find one that was called the lady of the morning and the evening."

"You studied too hard," Watch said. "The answer is simple."

"It is?" Adam asked. "What is it?"

"The lady referred to here is the planet Venus," Watch said. "The reference in the second line confirms that— 'The shadow of the white light of love shall falleth.' Venus is always associated with love. It is also the only planet in the sky capable of casting shadows on Earth. Few people realize that it can get that bright. But it only casts shadows when it is at its brightest, and when there is no moon. The first line also confirms it must be Venus because the planet is at its brightest when it is farthest from the sun, either as a morning or an evening star."

"When you say it is farthest from the sun, is it highest in the sky?" Adam asked, impressed.

"Yes," Watch said. "In a manner of speaking. Venus is highest—or tallest—when it is far from the sun from our perspective on Earth. Of course, it is always about the same distance from the sun. But from Earth, we see it swing close to and far from the sun."

"How often does this occur?" Adam asked.

Watch shrugged. "A couple times a year, or slightly more often. I'd have to study my books to know for certain. But one thing I do know—Venus is reaching its farthest point from the sun in the morning sky. If you get up early tomorrow, you'll see Venus before the sun rises. It'll be high in the eastern sky, and very bright."

"Is there a moon tonight?" Cindy asked. "Or early tomorrow morning, before it gets light?"

Watch paused. "No."

"Then this is a perfect time to look for the treasure," Sally said, excited.

"Hold on a second," Adam answered. "There are still a lot of clues here that we don't understand. Let's look at the other lines in the first verse. 'In a line of darkness on the door of the smallest. In a hidden spot on the tallest.'" Adam paused. "I assume this means that Venus casts a shadow on some object that points to a door that leads to the treasure."

Watch nodded. "I think it says that and more. It's full of information. I think the smallest is the smallest peak in the Teeth chain of peaks."

"But the hidden spot is on the tallest," Sally said. "That contradicts the previous line."

"Only at first glance," Watch said. "One of the peaks could be the tallest while still being the smallest."

"How?" Cindy asked.

"By being narrow," Watch said. "Even if the peak is tall, it could have the least mass."

"You're so smart, Watch," Cindy said with pleasure.

Sally patted Watch on the back. "Very good. I'm impressed. So now we have the first verse all figured out. But how far back in the mountains are the Teeth?"

Watch frowned. "Way back. We could drive part of the way there, but then we'd have to hike the rest."

"Can we get there in one day?" Adam asked.

"No," Watch said. "If we leave today, we'll have to camp out at least one night and hike the following day."

"But then Venus won't be at its highest point," Sally said. "We won't find what we're looking for."

"Venus won't shift that much in twenty-four hours," Watch explained. "I think these clues give us a window of opportunity of a few days." He paused. "But even if we can identify the correct peak, we might look for days for the right shadow. Unless . . ."

"Unless what?" Adam asked when his friend didn't complete his remark.

"Unless the light or shadow points out another marker," Watch said. "We can hope for that. But let's get back to the other verses. They have me stumped. Jewels that speak in dreams. Crystals that whisper words that are more than they seem. Leah, did your father describe the nature of the treasure?"

"No," she said cautiously. "Not exactly. He just said it was very ancient."

"The last verse speaks of an ancient pet," Sally said.

"And it tells us to beware of her," Adam said. "Maybe we should listen to what it says. She doesn't sound very friendly, not from her description here."

"*She* is probably dead," Sally said. "If the treasure is as old as Leah's father believed."

"Not necessarily," Watch said. "The line 'She who remembers old debts' implies that she lives for a very long time."

Cindy turned to Bryce. "You're really quiet. What do you think about what Watch said?"

Bryce nodded in admiration. "I'm stunned. I think he's figured the whole thing out."

"But I've only figured out the directions on the map," Watch said. "Not the other meanings. Have you any idea what this ancient pet could be?"

"No," Bryce said. "But like Sally, I believe it was something that lived a long time ago. I'm not worried about it."

"I can get a truck," Leah said. "And can drive us." She smiled suddenly. "This is exciting. If we do find the treasure, I think Watch should get an extra big share."

Watch flashed a rare smile. "I wouldn't mind one of those jewels that speaks in dreams."

Leah's smile shrank. "I'm sure we'll find something you like."

Cindy raised an important point. "I don't know about you guys, but I'm going to need time to convince my mom to let me go camping tonight. I won't tell her how far we're going. She'd worry too much."

Adam laughed. "If she only knew how far from home you've been other times, she wouldn't worry about this trip at all." He was referring, of course, to the times they had been in outer space. He added, "My parents will need to be convinced, too."

Sally stood. "My mom and dad like camping, and they'll be happy I'm spending the night with you guys. Don't forget to get your equipment together: sleeping bags, backpacks, and plenty of food and water."

Watch also stood. "I don't have to ask anyone where I can go."

Adam heard the sadness in his friend's voice. He knew that Watch's family was spread all across the country, although he didn't know why. Watch lived with some relative, but Adam forgot who.

"Doesn't anybody ever ask what you do?" Adam asked.

Watch shook his head. "Not usually."

Sally patted Watch on the back and smiled.

"But if you come home with a pile of treasure," she said, "all your relatives will talk to you plenty."

About the Author

CHRISTOPHER PIKE is the author of more than forty teen thrillers, including the Thirst, Remember Me, and Chain Letter series. Pike currently lives in Santa Barbara, where it is rumored he never leaves his house. But he can be found online at www.Facebook.com/ChristopherPikeBooks.